D0049246

MASTERMINDS

PAYBACK

MASTERMINDS

PAYBACK

GORDON KORMAN

BALZER + BRAY
An Imprint of HarperCollins*Publishers*

Balzer + Bray is an imprint of HarperCollins Publishers.

For information address HarperCollins Children's Books, a division of
HarperCollins Publishers, 195 Broadway, New York, NY 10007.
www.harpercollinschildrens.com

Library of Congress Control Number: 2016953028
ISBN 978-0-06-230005-8

17 18 19 20 21   PC/LSCH   10 9 8 7 6 5 4 3 2 1
❖
First Edition

For Leo Korman,
All–Around Mastermind

1

AMBER LASKA

The branch comes out of nowhere.

I don't even see it until it's too late to shout a warning. One second, we're riding down the river. The next, the limb catches Malik on the side of the head, pitching him off our makeshift raft into the water.

I don't hesitate. I can't. The current is so fast that I could be a quarter-mile downriver before I make up my mind. And anyway, it's a pretty selfish move. I've already lost Eli and Tori. If I lose Malik, too, I'm all alone.

I hit the water with a splash, and begin to swim upstream. It's a struggle with the river boiling all around me, and I'm grateful for the water polo training I got back in Serenity.

I never thought I'd be grateful for anything about growing up in that town.

Malik is moving toward me, carried by the current. He looks okay, except for a bloody gash behind his ear. I take hold of him in the classic Red Cross lifesaving position and head for shore.

He's shouting something, but I can't make it out over the roar of the river. What's he saying?

"You idiot, Laska! What are you doing?"

"Rescuing you!" I snarl back.

"I don't need rescuing! Why'd you jump off the raft?"

He's struggling against my grip. I pull harder for the riverbank. "We're stronger when we stick together!"

"Don't give me that Serenity baloney. Now we're *both* going to get caught!"

He wrestles free of my grasp, and the two of us swim ashore. We crawl through the reeds onto dry land and lie side by side, gasping and glaring at each other. I'm twice as mad at him as he is at me, because I know that if he could catch his breath, he'd be yelling at me.

He's right about one thing, though. Getting caught is a real danger. The Purple People Eaters saw us ride off on the river. When you escape from a commando team, you have to figure they'll be coming after you. Soon.

We scurry through the cover of the trees, staying low. After ten minutes, we come upon a two-lane highway with dirt shoulders. I'm about to step out, but Malik pulls me back.

"Use your brain," he hisses. "The next car around the bend could be one of their SUVs. I'm going up to see what I can see."

"Up?"

He starts climbing a huge old tree. I follow him. I've already jumped off a raft so I wouldn't be alone. I'm not about to stand there at the side of the road, waiting to get scooped up by Purples. It's a testament to what we've been through since escaping Serenity that neither of us thinks twice about scaling a thirty-foot oak. Running for your life does that to a person.

By the time we make it to the top, we wish we hadn't bothered. The two black SUVs carrying our pursuers are heading our way. They're hopscotching along the road, stopping periodically to send out teams of searchers into the woods. The lead car pulls over about three hundred yards short of us, and four men head into the trees.

We exchange a look of pure horror. Not only are they close, but we've trapped ourselves thirty feet in the air.

And then a pickup truck appears in the distance,

coming from the opposite direction, pulling a large white camper. It's going pretty fast, but it has to slow down to take the curve. In that instant, we both know what we're going to do. It's reckless and insane, but it's also our only option.

Malik is already hustling down to a lower branch, dragging me with him.

"I get it!" I whisper urgently. "Worry about yourself!"

About fifteen feet off the ground, a heavy branch extends out over the road. We crawl onto it, Malik in the lead. In a few seconds, the camper will pass directly beneath us.

"Jump early," I advise. "You know, to compensate for the motion of the—"

I never finish the sentence. He pushes me off the branch and lets go himself.

The drop is only about six feet, but it feels like a hundred miles. Maybe that's because, while we're falling, we have no idea if we're about to land catlike on the camper or with a splat on the pavement.

I hit the roof and flatten myself to the metal surface. Malik lands behind me a split second later. I look back with furious eyes.

He offers a slight shrug. "You said jump early."

I almost say, *I'm never going to forgive you for this!* I don't because this is at least the fifteenth thing I'm never going to forgive Malik for. Besides, he did care enough to push me, which means he's probably even more scared of being left alone than I am. Malik may look like a tough guy and a bruiser, but deep down, he's a big baby.

We stay pressed to the roof, keeping as low as possible, so we don't get to enjoy the moment when the camper sails by the SUVs. Too bad. I would have loved to laugh in their faces. Of course, that would have given us away. We have to be satisfied with the fact that they're going to search for hours, only to come up empty. I hope the mosquitoes are hungry tonight.

As the road straightens out, the camper speeds up again, and the wind begins to whip at our wet clothes. Suddenly, I'm freezing despite the heat, but that's far from the real issue. We're clinging to the roof like flies on a wall, with nothing to hang on to.

Malik inches his way up beside me. "Now what?" He has to shout to be heard over the wind and road noise.

"How should I know?" I shoot back. "This was your idea!"

"I only thought about getting away! I never made it this far!"

I look around. No luggage rack, no handhold, no bracing point. "Just hang on!" I manage.

In spite of everything we've been through, I've never been so scared in my life. Every curve threatens to hurl us off the camper. Every bump is sure to launch us into outer space. We lie flat, pressing our hands and feet against unyielding metal. Within minutes, our entire bodies ache with the effort. I'm a workout nut, but this is beyond anybody's physical capabilities.

Back in Serenity, I used to make a list every morning, planning out my entire day. If I could do that now, clinging to the roof in terror and agony, there would only be one item on it:

THINGS TO DO TODAY

- Don't let go!

The pickup just keeps driving, hauling our camper after it. It's putting miles between us and the Purples, but our daring escape isn't going to do us much good if we end up roadkill.

"I'm sorry!" Malik says suddenly.

"Huh?"

He's babbling now. "I'm sorry I made you jump! And— and for all that other mean stuff! If we get killed, you should know!"

Before I can reply, the truck's engine noise changes and we start to slow down. I dare to raise my head and see a weather-beaten old gas station coming up on the right.

"We're stopping!" I exclaim emotionally. I honestly don't believe we could have held on much longer.

"I was starting to think this bonehead was going camping in Oregon," Malik adds, sounding more like his old self.

The tires crunch as we pull off the road onto the gravel drive and come to a stop at the gas pump. The driver gets out of the pickup and heads around the back of the mini-mart to the restroom.

Malik and I don't wait for an engraved invitation. We crawl to the back of the camper and climb down the ladder. My arms are pure pain from shoulder to fingertips. When my feet touch the ground, I'm amazed that my rubbery legs hold me upright.

"I accept your apology," I whisper.

"What apology?" he growls. "Come on!"

We start for the cover of the wooded area behind the station when Malik suddenly freezes in front of the mini-mart. I look back to see what has captured his attention.

He's standing opposite a newspaper box, staring at a copy of today's *Dallas Morning News*. The headline is something about global warming, but I skip down the page to the story that's caught his eye:

GUS ALABASTER RELEASED FROM PRISON ON COMPASSIONATE GROUNDS

I recognize the name instantly, and just as instantly, I understand Malik's fascination with the news.

Gus Alabaster is one of the most notorious gangsters in American history.

He's also the criminal mastermind Malik is cloned from.

2

ELI FRIEDEN

Nice bracelet. Gold, studded with glittering stones.

"No price tag," I observe.

"Those are diamonds, Eli," Tori tells me. "Diamonds are expensive. Besides, check out how they've placed it in the display case. You can tell it's the star of the show. I wonder what it's worth."

I peer closer, my nose touching the hot glass of the jewelry store window. I'm not worried about attracting attention. The store is closed, and there's hardly anybody around. It's a broiling afternoon in Amarillo, Texas—the kind where sensible people stay inside in the air-conditioning. Our long bus ride north from Lubbock didn't buy us cooler weather.

I get what Tori's saying. It's like all the other pieces are in orbit around that bracelet. I'm not surprised she noticed. She has a great eye for detail that made her the best artist in our hometown, Serenity, New Mexico. I'm also not surprised that she zeroed in on the one item in the whole shop that would be most valuable to someone who steals it.

That comes from a part of Tori neither of us wants to think about.

To be honest, it all looks pretty expensive to me—rings, necklaces, earrings, and brooches; gold, platinum, gemstones. Not that we ever learned much about money in Serenity. Our parents took care of that, and they always seemed to have plenty. That was before we found out the whole town was fake, and the fakest thing about it was our parents. The creepy truth: they're scientists who've been studying us since the day we were born.

Of course, since leaving Serenity, we've learned a lot about money. Like you really can't survive without it. And we're running out of what little we had in the first place.

"No point wasting our time wondering how much we could get for a bracelet we're never going to touch in the first place." I point to a sign in the window: *THESE PREMISES PROTECTED BY APEX SECURITY.*

She steps back, scanning the store. When Tori looks at something, she takes in every detail, almost like she's

inhaling it. "Well, the alarm wires go through the door."
Then she points to a window in the second floor of the strip
mall shop. "But I bet there's a way in through the attic."

"The store has motion sensors," I point out.

It stops her for a second but not much longer. "See the
mail slot in the door? If we put a bird in through there —"

"You want to catch a bird?"

"I'm just thinking out loud. My mind does that on its
own. Doesn't yours?"

Well, yeah, but not like Tori's. Nobody's mind works
like Tori's. Okay, scratch that. Maybe one other person's—
and she's in jail right now.

"Anyway," she goes on, "the bird sets off the motion
sensor and triggers the alarm. But when the police come,
they see it's just a bird. So the owner turns off the motion
sensor until he can come back in the morning and chase the
bird out. And we have all night to get in from the upstairs.
Simple."

I stare at her—but it isn't Tori that I see. It's a convicted bank robber named Yvonne-Marie Delacroix,
presently serving a life sentence in a Florida prison. Tori
is an exact copy of her, right down to the DNA in every
one of her cells. Tori has never robbed a bank in her life.
Still, you have to figure that everything Yvonne-Marie is

capable of, Tori could be too.

"But we're not going to do that, right?" I say anxiously.

I have to ask, because I'm like Tori—I have the DNA of a criminal too. Not a bank robber. That would be a huge upgrade for me. But we've been breaking the law a lot lately. Don't get me wrong; we didn't bust out of Serenity to go on a crime spree. It's more like it took a crime spree to escape Serenity. And to keep us from getting caught and dragged back there.

Suddenly, Tori points. "Heads up!"

Across the parking lot, the front sliding doors of the supermarket part to reveal an elderly lady pushing a heavily loaded grocery cart.

Tori's off like a shot, but I'm right behind her. "It's *my* turn!" I hiss.

"It's *my* turn!"

"No way. You got the fat guy in the cowboy hat, remember?"

Tori backs off, and I approach the old woman just as she pops the cargo door of a Buick SUV.

"Here, ma'am, let me help you with that." I grab a bag and load it into the back of the Buick.

She beams at me. "Well, aren't you sweet!"

I'm not even a little bit sweet. I am an exact genetic

match for Bartholomew Glen, California's notorious Cross-word Killer. But on a ninety-eight-degree day, anyone who carries your parcels counts as sweet.

She tips me a dollar. A dollar! It would take more than a dollar's worth of soap and water just to wash the sweat off my poor sweltering body. I straggle back to Tori and we compare our take for the day.

"Fourteen dollars and fifty cents," I announce with a sigh. "For four hours in a parking lot."

"That bracelet could get us more," Tori puts in. "Then we could afford a hotel room. With real beds. And a bathroom."

"We're not criminals!"

"We kind of are," she reasons.

"Just because we're cloned from criminals doesn't mean we did any of the stuff they're in jail for," I insist.

That's what Serenity, New Mexico, turned out to be—not an actual town where people live and work and raise their kids, but a front for a twisted experiment called Project Osiris. Basically, the idea of Osiris is nature versus nurture. If you take evil people, raise them in the perfect community, and give them the perfect life, will they still turn out evil, because that's their nature? Or will they end up good, because that's how you've nurtured them to be?

You have to start an experiment like that from the very beginning, which means what you need is evil *babies*. Project Osiris cloned DNA samples from the worst criminal masterminds in the prison system and created us—exact copies of the scum of the earth. And they raised us as human guinea pigs to see if we could rise above our horrendous genes.

There are eleven of us, but only five escaped Serenity. One of us already turned out to be a traitor. Thanks to Hector Amani, we were almost recaptured four days ago. Tori and I got away by the skin of our teeth. The last we saw of Malik and Amber, they were being washed down white water by a brutal current. Even if they survived the river, they would have been in no shape to get away from their pursuers—our Serenity parents and their hired muscle, who we nicknamed the Purple People Eaters.

So it's up to us to stop Project Osiris. As tempting as it is to disappear and try to make new lives for ourselves, we can't turn our backs on the past. Six of our fellow clones are still under Osiris's thumb, with no idea of the truth about themselves. They're never far from our thoughts. When you grow up in such a tiny, isolated place, the handful of other kids in town are practically your brothers and sisters.

It seems impossible. I'm thirteen and Tori's only twelve.

Plus our story sounds totally nuts. How do we prove what's been done to us? Serenity's now a ghost town, all the evidence of the experiment burned to ashes.

The supermarket doors hiss open once more and a man steps out into the heat, struggling with two big bags.

Tori is already on the move. "My turn," she tosses over her shoulder at me.

I watch her catch up with the guy and take the bigger parcel from him—he won't let her carry both. They walk to his car, chatting amiably.

Tori loads the groceries into the man's trunk and he hands her a tip. The grin on her face is all the more remarkable because there's been so little to smile about these days. She pockets the bill and flashes me an open hand. That means five dollars, our biggest score of the day. I'm kind of insulted that nobody ever gives me that much. I guess Tori's a little stronger on charm than I am. That might be because her fake parents genuinely loved her—not like my dad, the ringleader of Osiris, who never had any use for me except as a lab rat.

A long dark sedan cruises across the blacktop and screeches to a halt right in front of Tori. The passenger door is flung open and a tall man wearing a black suit and sunglasses jumps out and grabs for her.

Too late the warning is torn from my throat. "Tori—run!"

She has another idea. She reaches into the grocery bag, pulls out a glass jar of pickles, and swings it at her attacker, catching him full in the face. He staggers back, dazed, his sunglasses askew. The pickle jar drops to the pavement and shatters.

I'm running flat out, desperate to reach her, my mind spinning with the horrible thought that Osiris has found us again. I don't recognize the man in sunglasses, but he could easily be one of the Purples.

"What do you think you're doing?" The shocked grocery shopper steps protectively in front of Tori.

The sedan's driver leaps out and shoves him to the pavement with a warning of, "Mind your own business, old man!"

Tori reaches into the trunk for another weapon. This time, she's not as lucky as she was with the pickle jar. She comes up with a long baguette and swings it like a baseball bat at the driver. With a cruel laugh, he allows her to club him with it a couple of times before yanking it from her hands.

Out of options, Tori flees. The driver springs after her. She's the fastest and most athletic of us—burglar DNA—

and I toy with the possibility that she can outrun him. He's got long legs, though, every stride of his matching two of hers. He's gaining fast.

I've got to help her, but what can I do? I'm fifty feet behind, and slower than both of them.

And then it comes to me—the sedan is just standing there with the motor idling and both doors open!

I jump in and throw the car in gear. I've driven before—Malik and I both taught ourselves so we could escape from Serenity. I'm just about to take off after them when a hand reaches across the front seat and grabs at my elbow. I forgot about the other guy—the one Tori hit with the pickle jar. His sunglasses are broken, and a big angry bruise is blooming in the center of his forehead.

I stomp on the accelerator and yank the wheel hard left. The car bursts forward, swerving violently. I feel the grip release from my arm, and when I glance over at my attacker, he's not there anymore. He's in the rearview mirror, twenty feet behind, still rolling on the blacktop.

Ahead, the first guy is almost up to Tori, so close he could grab her at any second. I roar alongside them, yelling through the open passenger door. *"Get in!"*

I see his mouth forming a shocked O as he realizes it's me and not his partner behind the wheel.

He grabs for the back of her T-shirt, but Tori shakes him off and flings herself into the car, landing with an "*oof!*" on the passenger seat.

He reaches for the door handle, just getting a finger on it. I stomp on the gas. The sedan leaps forward, leaving him in a heap on the pavement. I squeal out of the parking lot and take off down the street.

Tori manages to get herself upright and into her seat belt. "You're never going to believe this," she beams at me. "That guy tipped me five bucks!"

I almost steer into the ditch. "That's it? That's all you got out of what just happened? You were nearly kidnapped!"

"Well, yeah. There's that." She nods gravely. "Hey, you don't have to drive so fast. It's not like those two guys can catch us on foot."

I don't slow down. "They're not who I'm worried about. It's your big tipper—the one who isn't getting pickles for dinner tonight. For sure he's going to call the cops. I want to put some distance between us and that parking lot."

"Were those guys Purples?" she asks, her tone turning haunted. "Did you recognize them?"

"Not really," I admit, "but they weren't exactly standing still. Anyway, who else would be after us?"

"Four days," she moans. "That's all it took for them to

find us? How are we ever going to lose them?"

"Easy," I say. "We drive out of town and don't stop driving until we're a thousand miles from here."

"That's what they'll expect us to do," she muses thoughtfully. "And they know what car we're in. They might even be able to trace it by GPS."

GPS. That's my department. I have a knack for electronics. Phones and tablets and most computers have GPS antennas built into them, but I never thought about cars. My mind races. The transmitter would probably have to be on the roof, so the bulk of the vehicle doesn't block the signal.

We drive for another fifteen minutes and then I pull into a private-looking alley behind a row of stores, half of them boarded up. It takes only a few seconds paging through the owner's manual to find the antenna. It's the small fin-shaped thingamajig on top.

I climb up on the trunk and try to jam the flat end of the tire iron into the narrow space between the antenna's rubber weather stripping and the metal of the roof.

"Careful," Tori warns. "You're denting it."

"I'm not too worried about the resale value," I grunt, prying with all my might. "Especially considering whoever owns this car just tried to kidnap you. I can see the wires.

Have you got enough room to reach in and cut them?"

She brandishes the scissors from the glove compartment first aid kit. I hear snapping sounds. "I think that's all of them," she reports. "But how can we know for sure?"

We get back in and turn on the radio. Dead air.

We hit the road again, feeling a little bit safer. We still have to worry about the police in case the car is reported stolen.

We drive clear through the center of Amarillo, and it seems as if we're about to exit the town on the other side, since it looks like the suburbs again.

All at once, Tori barks, "Stop!" right in my ear.

I slam on the brakes, shaken. "What?"

"Look!" She points to a high fence with a sign: *NO TRESPASSING*.

"What about it?" I demand.

She indicates a second sign, newer than the first.

WAREHOUSE FOR LEASE
35,000 SQUARE FEET
AVAILABLE MAY 8TH

"Don't you see?" she says urgently. "It's what—the fifteenth? The sixteenth? It's hard to stay on top of the calendar when you're running for your life."

"Yeah, but what does that have to do with us?"

"Think," she insists. "If they just closed the place a week ago, and they're hoping to rent it again soon, it's probably not in bad shape. I'll bet they left the power on, and running water. And check out that door—" She nods toward the loading bay. The metal gate is up at least eight inches.

"It's not locked," I conclude.

"Right. We can get the car in there and lie low for a while. It'll give us a chance to breathe until we figure out what our next move is going to be."

I've got to hand it to Tori. When it comes to planning, Yvonne-Marie Delacroix could take lessons from her. The only skill I could have inherited through DNA is killing people. Or maybe composing crossword puzzles.

It's when we get out of the car that the flaw in her idea becomes clear. The front gate of the warehouse is tied shut by a chain, held in place by a padlock.

"What about *that*?" I ask. "And don't tell me you can pull out a hairpin and pick the lock."

"I wish." Tori studies the situation with that look on her face. "The chain is pretty rusty. Maybe we can break it with the tire iron."

"No way," I tell her. "That's solid metal."

"Was there a toolbox in the trunk?"

I shake my head. "Just the tire iron and the jack . . ."

My voice trails off. When you're changing a tire, you can use a jack to lift a whole car. If it's strong enough for that, maybe it's strong enough to break a metal chain.

We pop the trunk and dig out the jack, which is in the compartment with the spare tire. I examine it critically. It's a diamond shape, flat at first. But as you pump the handle, it grows taller and narrower.

Tori wedges the jack inside the tight chain that's holding the gate shut. Then I go to work with the handle. But instead of raising the body of a car, the expanding device is forcing the chain apart. As the loop is stretched to its limit, the ratcheting action becomes tighter, until I can barely budge it. I think of Malik, whose strong arm would come in handy just about now.

A panel truck rattles by on the uneven pavement, and Tori and I freeze like a couple of scared rabbits. Believe me, nothing has ever looked so much like breaking and entering as what we're doing right now. But the driver doesn't even glance in our direction, and soon he's gone.

The experience gives my arm a hidden reserve of power I never knew I had.

I was sweating before; now I'm as wet as if I'd been

dipped in a swimming pool. The cranking sound of the jack has slowed to a series of strained clicks.

Crack!

The chain snaps, whipping around in a lethal semicircle that would have taken off the tops of our heads if they had been in the way. The padlock slips off and hits the driveway with a clatter, still locked.

We unwrap the broken chain and the gate swings wide. I jump back in the car and drive it onto warehouse property. Tori pulls the gate shut behind me, and the two of us rush to wrap what's left of the chain into as close to its former position as possible. The padlock is intact, but we can remove the impediment any time we want to. The important thing is no one can tell that the gate has been opened unless they examine it closely.

Next order of business: hiding the car. We turn our attention to the partially open loading bay door. I try to lift it higher, and can't budge it.

Tori is undeterred. She rolls through the opening, and a few seconds later the door is rising on an electric motor. We're in.

I ease the car inside, and we lower the door behind it. Safe—or at least as safe as we can possibly be, considering our situation.

The warehouse is dim, but the lights work, and so does the air-conditioning. It's the kind of comfort we haven't seen for a long time. The bus tickets from Lubbock ate up most of our cash, and we've been rationing what little we have left so we can feed ourselves. Our career as grocery carriers isn't exactly bringing in the big bucks. We've been sleeping in a shelter made of old grocery cartons outside the supermarket, in a place where the overnight low temperature is a steamy ninety degrees.

The warehouse is a vast soaring space with towering steel shelving units that stretch as far as the eye can see. There's a small office area with better lighting, upholstered furniture, and even a TV in the break room. The couches look pretty enticing, sleep-wise. And there are bathrooms—real bathrooms. I'm psyched about that, but not half as much as Tori. The executive office even has a shower.

"This'll do," she decides with a satisfied smirk.

It's good to see her happy, although I can't help but think about how far we've fallen. We had the best of everything in Serenity—large, comfortable homes, pools, every convenience and luxury you can think of. Of course, we were experiment subjects then, and we aren't anymore.

Fugitives, maybe, hunted like animals. But there's a lot to be said for freedom.

"I wonder what this warehouse was used for," I muse.

Tori steps into the main area and digs through a carton on the nearest shelf. She comes up with a box of Girl Scout Cookies.

"No way!" I exclaim.

She tears open the container and we're halfway through the shortbreads before even coming up for air. Nothing ever tasted better.

"Things are finally starting to go our way," she mumbles, her mouth full.

"Definitely," I agree, scanning the array of cartons on the shelf. Thin Mints, Caramel deLites, Peanut Butter Patties, Cranberry Citrus Crisps, Rah-Rah Raisins, Toffeetastic—it goes on and on. I take in the lofty heights of the storage units, boxes upon boxes, all the way to the forty-foot ceiling. "We could be here for centuries and never run out."

"Amber wouldn't be able to handle this," Tori reflects. "You know how crazy she gets about eating right."

The thought of our lost friends takes some of the celebration out of our feast. If Malik and Amber were recaptured by Purples, it means any chance they have is in our hands. And where are we? Hunkered down in an old warehouse inhaling Girl Scout Cookies.

That's the real problem. Up until now, we were always working toward a goal. First it was escaping Serenity, but that was just the beginning. Next it was finding Tamara Dunleavy, billionaire cofounder of Project Osiris—only to have her deny she knows anything about it. Last, it was connecting with C. J. Rackoff, one of the Osiris DNA donors. We made a deal with him, even broke him out of prison, and were betrayed by him and Hector, his clone.

If Tamara Dunleavy is a dead end, and so are the criminal masterminds we're cloned from, what's our next move?

Sure, we have a lifetime's supply of cookies, but that's not what we really need.

We need a future.

3

MALIK BRUDER

When I get my first glimpse of the Chicago skyline, I know I'm not in Happy Valley anymore.

Okay, we've seen cities before. This train alone passed through Oklahoma City, Kansas City, and St. Louis.

Dinky compared to this.

Don't get me wrong. Any city—and 99.9 percent of all towns—is better than Serenity, New Mexico, the tiniest, stupidest, fakest pimple on the hairy butt of humanity. The fact that it's not there anymore—or at least that it's abandoned—makes the world a much better place.

Too bad Laska's missing the first view of all these skyscrapers.

We slow down and the announcement comes that the next stop will be Chicago's Union Station.

I get out of my seat, walk to the bathroom at the end of the car, and give the special knock—three, two, and one.

Amber slides the door open a couple of inches.

"Chicago," I tell her. "And wait till you see it."

She comes out, giving me her nastiest face. "Next time, *I* get the real ticket and *you* ride in the toilet."

We only had enough money for one train fare, so one of us had to be the stowaway. I look older, at least old enough to be traveling on my own. Amber had to tough it out.

I wonder if it's worth the nagging I'm in for. "You talk like you spent the last two days in there. Most of the trip you were right next to me. It was just when the conductor was nosing around that you had to get lost."

"Just take me off this train," she mutters. "People are looking at me like I belong in the hospital. Nobody spends so much time in the bathroom."

"Maybe you think we should have stayed in Texas with the Purples," I challenge.

She relents a little. She knows as well as I do that Gus Alabaster is our only lead, our one connection to the beginning of Project Osiris, before we were born. All the other criminals we were cloned from are either in prison or dead. Except for C. J. Rackoff, of course. The only reason he's not behind bars is because we broke him out. And he stabbed us in the back for it. Stupid to trust Rackoff; stupid to trust anybody connected to Hector. Or maybe I've got that backward, since Hector is Rackoff's clone.

Anyway, a few days ago, Gus Alabaster—my guy—was released from jail. His sentence isn't over, or anything like that. He still has eleven years to go on the tax evasion charge they finally hung on him. But he has cancer, and the doctors say he hasn't got much longer to live. So they let him out so he can spend his last days at home.

I smuggle Amber safely off the train in spite of the conductor's very suspicious frown. Pretty soon we're walking around downtown Chicago, staring at the crowds and the buildings and the elevated trains, and the river running right through the center of town. I can tell it's a lot bigger and more happening than Denver, the other major city we've been in. You can just feel the energy in the sights and sounds and sheer thrum of the place. I love it.

But there's a problem. How do you find one dying gangster in a city of millions like this? It's not Happy Valley, where you could knock on every door in town in twenty minutes, half an hour, tops.

Amber has a suggestion. "Why don't we go to the library?"

"We haven't got time to *read*," I tell her. "This guy

could kick it before we ever get a chance to talk with him."

"A library is all about *information*," she insists. "Maybe his address is on file somewhere."

I feel a stirring of hope. Back in Serenity, Amber's mom was our teacher. Her fake mom, I mean. The point is, Amber was brought up in a house that was big on learning.

The Serenity Public Library was a closet full of books in the town hall. The library we get directed to looks more like an Asian palace done in red brick. There are about a gazillion books in there, but we fall on the computers.

Laska is getting a little teary. "Computers make me think of Eli."

I know she's also worrying about Tori, her best friend. I consider my own best friend—Hector. If he was here right now, I'd push his teeth down his traitorous throat. Which means I probably have more in common with Gus Alabaster than I thought.

Anyway, the reason computers bring Eli to mind is he's a genius with them, which is especially amazing for a guy who grew up in a place where the internet was all bogus. But we don't need a genius—we just need to look up everything we can find about Alabaster. Between Laska and me, surely we can manage that.

We've researched Alabaster online before, but the

Chicago Public Library has a lot more stuff—a vast database of every newspaper and magazine article ever written about the guy from the time of his first arrest in 1963, at the age of fifteen.

We pore over the material, searching for the one thing we need to know. He's an international playboy with homes all over the world, but the government took a lot of that back when they found him guilty. He only has one residence left—and it's right here in Chicago.

"But what's the address?" Amber seethes in frustration.

A sharp "Shhh!" comes from around the library.

She drops her voice but her face is pinched. "Gus Alabaster is horrible! If even half of all this is true, he deserves to die in jail and then be brought back to life so he can die in jail again!"

"Really? I think he sounds kind of cool."

She glares at me. "If you'd skip over the parts about the movie stars he dated and the yachts he bought, and read about the crimes he committed, you'd see the kind of monster he is."

How am I supposed to take that? I mean, I'm not Gus Alabaster, but I'm an exact copy. "At least he's not a terrorist," I tell her, "like who you got *your* DNA from."

She's got no answer for that.

Two pointless, wasted hours later, we give up and leave the library.

I slam my fist into a mailbox. "I didn't spend two days on a train to *not* find my guy!"

Amber sighs. "If his address isn't in that library, it's nowhere. The only people who know where Gus Alabaster is are his neighbors, poor unfortunate souls. I'll bet it was a nasty shock to them to look out the window and see the psychopath next door moving back in."

I stop in my tracks. "You know, that's not exactly true. Somebody else knows where he is—somebody who should be pretty easy to find."

"Who?"

"The cops. He has to inform the police of his where-abouts at all times—it said that in the newspaper."

She stares at me. "You've got to be joking! We can't go to the police. For all we know, Project Osiris has put out a bulletin about us across the whole country!"

"It's still a risk we have to take," I argue. "Yeah, Osiris might have reported us—but that was over a thousand miles away. We're no more likely to show up in Chicago than we are in Seattle, or Miami, or Bangor, Maine. We'll use fake names, and if any cop gets too nosy, we'll get out of there."

She's not convinced. "But why would the Chicago Police Department give out confidential information to two random kids just because they ask for it?"

"Because we're not random," I explain. "I'm Gus's long-lost son, and I've come to say an emotional good-bye to my dying father before he bites it."

"But Gus Alabaster doesn't have a son," she points out.

"That's the long-lost part. And everybody has to believe me because of the family resemblance. I must look like him. I *am* him." I add, "You don't have to come with me."

"Oh, I'm coming with you, all right," she says quickly. "Someone has to keep you out of trouble."

We've been to a police station before—in Denver, soon after we escaped from Happy Valley. We were so clueless back then. We're wiser now, but it's still scary to see all those squad cars parked outside and all those uniforms coming and going. We're still not sure where we stand in the outside world. Human cloning is illegal, but does that mean it's against the law to be a clone? We can't even be positive that we count as 100 percent human.

It's the busiest place I've ever seen in my life, noisier even than the train station, with an underlying thrumming caused by hundreds of fingers on computer keyboards. We sit in the waiting room next to some guy who has an arrow through his forearm—I kid you not. There are people in expensive suits and people in rags. One older man is wrapped in what looks like a kind of homemade diaper. A girl about college age is swatting at imaginary flies. Everybody's sweating. It doesn't smell so great in here. Then again, Laska and I are probably pretty rancid ourselves after two days on a train. We're still wearing the same clothes we washed down the river in, and wind-dried on top of a speeding camper.

When I finally get called, I give my name as Bryan Jackson—Bryan after the Purple People Eater who is married to our old water polo coach, and Jackson after Jackson Hole, Wyoming, where Tamara Dunleavy lives. I'm trying to give my story to a desk sergeant who is about as interested as a hibernating bear. The only time his ears perk up is when I drop the name Gus Alabaster.

"You mean the gangster?"

"He's my father," I resume the telling, "even though we've never met. He doesn't even know I exist. Mom only told me I was his son when she read that he hasn't got long to live."

The desk sergeant stops making notes and looks up at me. "What exactly is the nature of your complaint?"

"I'm not complaining about anything. I just need Gus Alabaster's address so I can go over there and meet him before he dies."

"So no actual crime has been committed," he concludes.

I shake my head. "No crime. I just need the address."

"We don't do that here. Sorry, kid. Next!"

Diaper Man gets up and heads for the desk. What can I do? I turn to walk away, utterly defeated. But before I can take a step, Laska rushes over and pushes me back into the chair.

"Aren't you going to help him?" she shrills at the desk sergeant, her face flaming bright red. "Don't you even care?"

The cop leans back in his chair. "And you are?"

"All he wants to do is have a moment with his dying father!" Tears—real tears—are streaming down her cheeks. "And there's a time limit for that, you know!"

The desk sergeant's half-closed eyes pop wide open. He's probably seen it all working this job, but a crying girl turns out to be the one thing he doesn't know what to do with. And I've got to hand it to Laska. As soon as she sees she's spooking the guy, she switches on the full waterworks.

He hustles to his feet. "Uh—follow me."

And we're led into an interview room.

"Listen," I whisper when we're alone. "When the next guy comes, let me do all the talking, okay?"

She's insulted. "If it wasn't for me, you'd be out on the street now!"

"And you were awesome," I agree. "But from here on in it's my show."

"Fine," she concedes.

I can't help noticing that after all that sobbing, her eyes are completely dry.

Eventually, a plainclothes officer with a bushy mustache comes in and sits down opposite us. "I'm Detective Rollins, OCU—that's Organized Crime Unit. Now what's all this about you wanting to see Gus Alabaster?"

"He's my dad," I tell him. "I just found out. And if I don't see him soon, I'll never get a chance." Remembering Amber's success, I act as emotional as I can. I even try to squeeze out a tear or two, but it doesn't happen. It's my Alabaster DNA working against me.

The cop folds his arms and peers at me. "Does your mother know you're here?"

The question catches me off guard. My mother—the scientist who pretended to be my mother. She loved me. I know it. She did a lousy thing with Project Osiris, but I'm positive she came to love the poor little clone they gave her to raise.

Detective Rollins pops a tissue out of a box and hands it to me. I'm bewildered for a moment. Then I realize that I'm crying, just like Amber did before. Only with me, it's the real thing.

"Want me to call her for you?" the cop persists.

I shake my head, dabbing at my eyes.

Rollins nods. "I get it. Your mom hits you with this bombshell, but she won't take you to him. So you and your little friend here set out to go find him on your own. Is that about right?"

I have myself back under control, because I've got to be ready for what comes next. This guy Rollins is no dope, and if he asks for my mother's name, address, or telephone number, I've got to be careful what I say.

Instead, he says, "I can't tell you what you want to know."

Amber speaks up for the first time. "Why not?"

Rollins stays focused on me. "Look, kid, for what it's worth, I believe you. I've pulled some of the old mug shots on Alabaster, and you could be the guy's twin. But it's department policy. We can't pass out confidential information."

"Not even to immediate family?" Amber wheedles.

He's still talking just to me. "Listen, you really want to

meet Gus Alabaster? Talk to your mom. She'll contact his people. If he wants to see you, he'll set up a meeting." He pauses. "But if you really want to do yourself a favor, forget you ever found out he's your father. He's a bad guy."

We walk out of there, dragging our feet. Laska feels so bad for me that she slips her hand into mine. I drop it like a hot potato. I don't need consolation; I need an address. Otherwise we came all the way to Chicago for nothing.

We're just outside the precinct house when the original desk sergeant comes waddling through the double doors, his handcuffs clinking at his belt. He hands me a folded scrap of paper.

When I regard him questioningly, he mumbles, "My old man passed when I was about your age."

I look at the paper. There are two words on it: *RAMSEY ROAD*.

"Alabaster's address!" Laska whispers, her voice tense with excitement.

"But what number?" I call.

"Don't worry." He tosses the answer over his shoulder without turning around. "You'll know."

The desk sergeant is right. The minute the taxi makes the turn onto Ramsey Road, we do know.

Ramsey is a short street in northwest Chicago, lined with small, neat, wood-frame homes. Midway down the block, on what must be four regular lots, someone has built the Taj Mahal. Well, not really, but it's a gigantic stone mansion that overshadows everything else around it.

"It's that house over there," I direct the driver. "The big one."

"Kind of stands out in the neighborhood," the guy observes.

"Yeah." I'm strangely proud of the place, almost like I built it myself.

"Tasteless" is Laska's opinion.

"Are you crazy? It must be worth a fortune!"

"No one needs a house that big," she says disapprovingly. "And it's even worse to put it on a modest little street to rub it in people's faces how much richer he is than everybody else."

"That's the whole point of being rich," I explain patiently. "What good is it if nobody's jealous?"

We pay for the taxi, noting that we don't have enough money left for a return ride downtown. If Alabaster kicks us out, we're going to have to find a bus or something. It's kind of pointless to worry about transportation when you've got nowhere to go anyway. This out-of-place palace—and the sick gangster inside it—is our only lead.

The sun is setting, so we're in the shadow of the house as we start up the front walk. It's also the tallest home around, not just the biggest. There are two slightly overdressed men in their twenties sitting at a table on the porch, playing cards. Spying us, they interrupt their game and stand.

Beside me, Laska intones, "These guys don't seem the type who'll believe us when we tell them about Project Osiris."

"Good point," I agree. "I'm going to stick with the long-lost-son story until we get to see Alabaster himself."

When we reach the steps between two huge stone lions, the men get up and block our way. "Private property, kids," says the taller one.

There's something about the way he says it—flat, disinterested, yet there's no question that it's a threat. Like it makes no difference to him whether or not he has to drag me, kicking and screaming, back to the sidewalk. For some reason, it doesn't scare me, not even when I notice the bulge in his sports jacket that's probably a holstered gun.

"We're here to see Mr. Alabaster," Amber announces.

"That's not going to happen," the shorter guard deadpans.

"It's important," I say. "Tell him it's his son."

The two look at each other. "Nice try. The boss has got no kids."

"He has me. He just doesn't know it yet. I only found out myself a few days ago." I add, "How do you think Mr. Alabaster will feel if he finds out you sent away his only son?"

They withdraw a few steps and hold a whispered conversation.

"Wait here," the taller one orders, and disappears into the house.

He returns a few minutes later with an older man, a bald guy in shirtsleeves, who sees me, and halts in his tracks. "Holy—" He catches himself. "Excuse my French. You look just like him."

The guards stare at him in amazement, and he snaps, "Idiots! You think the boss was always old and sick? This kid's the spitting image! What's your name, son?"

"Bryan Jackson," I say, going back to the story I used at the police station. "And this is Amber, my—friend."

"She stays here," the bald guy decides. "Tommy, get her a lemonade or something. Bryan, follow me."

And I'm on my way to meet the notorious gangster whose DNA was the blueprint for me.

The house has fifteen-foot ceilings and was decorated

by somebody who really liked gold. There are huge gold-framed mirrors and a spiral staircase with a gold banister, topped by a chandelier of shiny crystal and gold. It's super-fancy, but even I can tell that it's over the top.

Baldy escorts me into a gigantic sitting room with—guess what—gold wallpaper and gold drapery on the windows. At the far end there's an old man in a wheelchair surrounded by medical equipment—tubes, wires, and a heart monitor flashing graphs and numbers. A uniformed nurse stands at a discreet distance.

My first thought is: *No way this is Gus Alabaster! He's nothing like the pictures from the newspaper files!* The man looks a hundred years old, feeble, and so skinny that his head is just a skin-wrapped skull. Then it occurs to me—they don't let healthy people out of jail on compassionate grounds. This person is at death's door. I don't doubt he's a bad guy like the cop said. But I can't help feeling sorry for him.

We come closer and Baldy performs the introduction. "Boss—this is the kid. This is Bryan."

The old man looks me up and down. To my shock, I recognize his eyes, even though they're red-rimmed and bloodshot. They're *my* eyes.

In a papery voice, he asks, "Who's your mother?"

It's the one question I'm not prepared for. My mind is

whirling with plans on how I'm going to get to the subject of DNA and clones and Project Osiris. It never occurred to me that I'd have to back up the lie that originally got me in the door. But if I hit him with all that clone stuff now, he'll think I'm a crackpot and have me thrown out. Or worse.

No. The only way to make this work is to stick with the long-lost-son story until I'm comfortable enough with him to give the old guy the truth.

Fighting panic, I channel Tori, the best natural liar I know. She always said in order to sound natural, you use as much of the truth as you can. "Ellen Jackson," I manage, using the first name of my Serenity mother.

"Got a picture?"

"Not with me."

He frowns. "I don't remember her."

A loud bark makes me jump. A large German shepherd lopes into the room, galloping straight for me. I'm thinking I'm dead—that Alabaster gets rid of all his fake children by feeding them to this monster. The dog leaps and I put up my hands in a futile attempt to protect myself.

The shepherd lands with a huge paw on each of my shoulders and proceeds to lick my face, his grizzled muzzle tickling my chin, his tail wagging.

A weak cackle comes from the wheelchair. "You're

family, all right. Counselor hates everybody."

As if to prove this point, the dog stops licking me for a moment to throw a contemptuous bark at Baldy.

"He was just a pup when I got him," Alabaster goes on. "He's an old man now, with one foot in the grave—not that I'm anyone to talk. But he remembered me, even after fourteen years in the can. Half licked my face off. Almost took out all these tubes and wires and contraptions."

The dog is sliming me big-time, and he doesn't smell so great either. I'm afraid to twist away though, because the old gangster seems to think this is proof we're related. Right now, I might be the only person in the world who knows that a dog can't tell the difference between you and your clone. So, in your face, Project Osiris. You may be the scientists, but I scooped you on this.

Nobody had any pets in Happy Valley, except for the occasional lizard or scorpion in a bottle. That never struck me as weird until this minute. Maybe Osiris felt that animals would interfere with their precious experiment, like being slobbered on by some mutt might bring out the criminal mastermind in your personality.

Baldy finally comes to my rescue, grabbing the dog by the back of the collar and pulling him off me. Counselor nearly bites his head off. "You'd think he'd be a little more grateful by now. I've only been feeding him for fourteen years."

"Loyalty," Alabaster approves.

"More like fear." The words are out before I have a chance to think about what I'm saying.

They stare at me.

"You know—" I backpedal. The damage is already done, so I've got no choice but to finish the thought and hope for the best. "Because it's no good for your health to be the guy who got rid of the boss's dog."

Baldy is regarding me in genuine horror, and I'm thinking I've really blown it. I've insulted Chicago's toughest mobster in his own home. Best-case scenario, I'll be thrown out, and so much for any chance of learning about the early days of Project Osiris. And that's if I'm lucky. If I'm unlucky—my mind returns to that cop from the Organized Crime Unit: *He's a bad guy.* A bad guy who knows he's dying, which means he's got nothing to lose.

All at once, Alabaster brays a raspy laugh that finishes in spasm of coughs. "I love this kid, Lenny! Where'd you find him?"

Baldy—*Lenny*—manages a slight shrug while struggling to restrain the dog. "He and his girlfriend just walked in off the street."

"Girlfriend?" Alabaster grins, stretching his pale skin even tighter across the bones of his face. "You're even more like me than me! A regular chip off the old block!"

I cringe. He can't know how close that is to the truth. A chip off the old block—as in they took a chip off him to make me. Aloud, I tell him, "She's not my girlfriend."

He doesn't believe me. "That's exactly what I would have said. Don't snow me, Bryan. You're talking to the master. How old are you?"

"Fifteen," I lie. I'm actually thirteen, but it has to make sense that he could have fathered me before going in to prison.

"Where are you from?"

"New Mexico," I reply, sticking to Tori's maximum truth rule. "I never knew who my real father was until my mom heard on TV that you were—about your medical situation."

"That I'm about to croak," the old gangster amends. "Pointless to sugarcoat it."

"I wanted to meet you, and she said no," I go on. "So I took off."

He nods understandingly. "I left home around your age too. My old man kicked me out. Said I'd never amount to anything. By the time I was eighteen, I'd made more money than he'd ever see in his whole life."

Lenny has a question. "How did you find us? Where'd you get the address?"

"From the cops."

He's incredulous. "And they gave it to you?"

"Not all of them," I admit. "But it only takes one."

"To protect and to serve," Alabaster snorts in disgust, dislodging the oxygen feed from his nostrils. He reinserts it with a trembling hand and turns back to me. "Well, Bryan, I know it's been a long trip, but I'm glad you came. The thought of my own kid marching into the police station and demanding my address—it's classic. And then showing up here. You've got some guts, I'll say that for you. Runs in the family."

He dissolves into another coughing fit, a longer one this time. Numbers on the electronic monitor change rapidly, racing up and down again. At a beep of warning, the nurse comes over and covers the patient's mouth and nose with a breathing mask. After a few more seconds, his respiration stabilizes.

Alabaster himself removes the mask, and shoos the nurse back to her former position. "All right, kid. You wanted to meet me. So you've met me. Now what? What are your plans?"

I hesitate. No way can I hit him with Project Osiris and the clone thing now—especially not after my whole sob story about running away from home to come find him.

So I shake my head. "I don't have any."

"Where are you staying in town?" he persists.

"It isn't your problem," I tell him.

"It *is* my problem," Alabaster shoots back with surprising force. The voice is still reedy, but there's authority, even vigor behind it. For the first time, I see how this weakened shell of a person used to be what the newspapers called the most successful gangster in American history.

"You're my kid," he goes on. "You're staying with me. Lucky for you, a dying man doesn't take up much space. Your girl too. Bring her in here. I want to meet her."

Lenny has a concern. "Boss, putting up runaways—the cops'll make trouble for us if they get wind of it. They're already bent out of shape that the judge sprung you."

"Let them," scoffs the old gangster. "My last stop was Joliet and my next is a hole in the ground. What can they do to me—arrest me again?"

That's why, a few minutes later, I'm back outside. Laska is pressed up against the porch rail, trying to put as much distance as possible between herself and the two goons, who have resumed their card game. She's clutching a full glass of lemonade like it's the head of a cobra, and if she relaxes her grip it'll swallow her whole. She's cloned from a notorious terrorist, but she can be a total Goody Two-shoes sometimes, with a holier-than-thou attitude that drives me crazy. As if drinking a gangster's lemonade makes you an accessory to everything he did.

"How did it go?" she whispers.

"Not bad," I reply at regular volume. "In fact, we're moving in."

Her eyes widen into saucers.

"My dad wants to get to know his long-lost son," I explain. "So he invited us to stay with him for a while. Come on, he wants to meet you."

As Lenny leads us down the hall of gold-framed mirrors, Amber sidles up to me. "Did he tell you anything about Project Osiris?"

I shake my head. "I didn't get that far. He still thinks I'm his kid. Oh, and one more thing. If anybody asks, you're my girlfriend."

"What—?"

Her protest goes no further than that, because Lenny opens the door and ushers us into the room, and she's face-to-face with a dying crime boss. I feel bad about blindsiding her this way. But not so bad, since watching Laska squirm is at least a little bit fun.

I've got to hand it to her, though. She pulls it off, somehow making her expression of loathing come across as respect.

Alabaster appraises her critically and turns to me. "You like them wild, huh? I approve."

Wild? I regard Amber as if for the first time. She was wanted by the cops back in Denver, so she had to cut her long blond hair and dye it black. Now her natural color is growing out, and there are splashes of dark, fair, and even some red where the dye is fading. It's a very punk look after a dunk in the river and an eighty-mile-an-hour blow-dry on top of a speeding camper. What a change from the prim and proper Serenity girl she used to be.

She says, "Pleased to meet you, Mr. Alabaster."

"Call me Gus." He goes into another coughing fit, but waves away the nurse as he gets himself under control. "When they sprung me from Joliet, who would have thought I was headed for a family reunion? Who would have thought I was headed for a family?"

And I'm the guy who has to tell him it isn't true.

Lucky me.

4

TORI PRITEL

I guess I can't really call myself an artist anymore. I haven't so much as sketched anything since we left Serenity (which feels like two lifetimes ago). My parents made me a fully equipped studio in our attic, but that's hundreds of miles away in an empty, dead town that was never real in the first place.

One thing has stayed with me, though—my eye for detail. I notice things that other people don't. For example, a stroller, a small bike, and a Big Wheel in the open carport means there are kids in this house. And kids like cookies.

I ring the doorbell. The woman who answers has a baby on her hip and a cell phone at her ear. Perfect. Just busy enough not to ask too many questions.

"Hi, ma'am. I'm selling Girl Scout Cookies to support

my troop. Would you like to buy some?"

Amazingly, she's able to fish out a ten-dollar bill without putting down either the phone or the kid. "Have you got Thin Mints?"

That's something I've learned in the past hour. Everybody loves the Thin Mints. Luckily, I've got a huge supply of all flavors. (I happen to have an entire warehouse at my disposal.) Obviously, I can't bring the whole warehouse with me. But Eli found a loading dolly that we piled up, and I've been selling the stuff around the neighborhood. And business is booming.

It definitely beats carrying groceries.

I hand over her Thin Mints and her change. She's about to close the door, when she asks suddenly, "Shouldn't you be in your uniform?"

I give her my best smile, the one with all the teeth. "They have mercy on us in the summer. The outfit's really hot. Thanks again!"

In Serenity they taught us that honesty was the most important of the Three Essential Qualities of Serenity Citizens (honesty, harmony, and contentment). Here in the outside world, though, a lie comes to me as easily as breathing. It used to make me sad, but now I'm so focused on survival that I'll say anything to anybody. Staying free is all that matters.

I head down the walk toward the next house, pushing the dolly ahead of me. The stacks of cookie boxes are a lot shorter than when I started out. And there's no mistaking the thick wad of bills bulging in my pocket. I must have over three hundred dollars. If Yvonne-Marie Delacroix knew there was so much money in Girl Scout Cookies, she might have given up robbing banks.

The thought makes me laugh out loud, but there's really nothing funny about this. I'm selling stuff that's not mine to sell, which is a kind of stealing too. The whole purpose of Project Osiris was to see if evil kids would still grow up to be evil adults if you give them the perfect upbringing. I don't have to turn into Yvonne-Marie Delacroix. I'm her already. For sure, the keen powers of observation I'm so proud of were useful to Yvonne-Marie in casing banks and finding weak spots in security systems.

On the other hand, Eli and I need money if we're going to eat—although we've both put away so many cookies in the last two days that we've probably stored up enough calories to hibernate until Christmas. Fine, we'll buy clothes, then. We're both wearing the same stuff we escaped in, and it's getting plenty ripe. (We obviously can't keep a low profile if people smell us half a block away.)

I guide my rolling inventory up the next walk. This house isn't any bigger, but it's beautifully maintained. The paint is fresh. The windows gleam. The landscaping is perfect. There are two nice cars in the driveway. Let's hope they like cookies. They can certainly afford to buy a lot of them.

A kid opens the door—a girl a year or two younger than me.

"Hi," I greet her. "I'm selling Girl Scout Cookies."

Her eyes narrow. "You're not part of our troop."

Uh-oh. "I'm from the north side of town. My mom dropped me off here because our neighborhood is all cookied out."

"It's the wrong time," she says with a frown. "All the big sales were last month. Where's your ID badge? You're not even wearing your uniform."

"Well, it's so hot—"

Before I can stammer out an excuse, the mom appears behind her. "What's going on?"

"It's our annual fund drive," I explain smoothly.

"I'm the troop leader for Troop three twenty-eight," she tells me. "I know all the troops around here. No one has an annual fund drive. Where did you get those cookies?"

I may not be Yvonne-Marie Delacroix, but I know when it's time to disappear. I roll the dolly into the doorway, blocking it, and take off like a jackrabbit. My career as a Girl Scout is officially over.

I cut through backyards, hurdling lawn chairs and vegetable gardens and vaulting over fences. It's a talent I inherited from my DNA donor, along with my powers of observation—not just the athletic ability to escape, but also the instinct to be stealthy about it, rather than just taking the easy route and fleeing down the street. I have no idea if that troop leader will call the police over grand theft Girl Scout Cookies. Still, I can't take the chance of leading anybody back to the warehouse—especially not the police. There's a car there that really is a grand theft. And if the cops start looking into Eli and me, no good will come of that.

Where the neighborhood ends, I dash through a scrap-metal yard and cross the main road, heading for our warehouse. I don't hear any police sirens, which is a good sign. But that doesn't mean the troop leader isn't on the phone right now, reporting me to the Girl Scout head office. I obviously need to disappear, and fast.

The sight of the warehouse gives my feet wings. I blast

up to the gate and reach out to unwind the padlock chain. The shock is like a physical blow.

The chain is loose, hanging down to the pavement. I know for a fact that I rewound it carefully after letting myself out with the dolly of cookies. Eli would have done the same.

Someone has opened the gate.

5

ELI FRIEDEN

I have a knack for computers.

It doesn't make sense. Tori has a lot of talents that probably trace back to the bank robber she's cloned from. Malik is tough and intimidating, even a bit of a bully, just like a mob boss would be. Amber is passionate, reckless, and absolutely unstoppable once she decides on a course of action. One by one, none of these traits are so bad; together, they describe Mickey Seven, the terrorist whose DNA created Amber. Even Hector is an echo of the embezzler and con artist C. J. Rackoff—super-smart, but in a figuring-the-angles, untrustworthy way.

But I'm cloned from Bartholomew Glen, the notorious Crossword Killer. Trust me, it's not a fun thing to know about yourself. Every flash of temper, every time I get angry, or frustrated, or impatient, I have to wonder if that's my Glen DNA coming out. Not only did Bartholomew Glen murder nine people—he made a *game* out of it. He taunted the police with clues to the killings in the form of elaborate crossword puzzles.

How does that translate to being good with computers?

Not that I'm complaining. My skills helped us discover the truth about ourselves and Project Osiris back in Serenity, and they've saved our necks more than once since we broke out. Again and again they've provided us with valuable information to help us survive in the outside world.

That's why I'm sitting in the office section of the warehouse, hacking into the Amarillo Police Department's website. It takes me just a few minutes to access their stolen vehicle reports. I scan down the long list, looking for the car that's parked on the other side of the wall, amid the tall storage units of Girl Scout Cookies.

I check and double check. It's not there.

I try again, this time searching by license plate number. Still nothing.

I frown. I guess people who try to kidnap girls in parking lots don't want too much involvement with the police. They haven't reported the theft, but that doesn't mean they never will. They're probably trying to find the car on their own first.

The question remains: Who are they? Purple People Eaters? Nobody else knows we're—special. If it isn't someone from Osiris, who else could it possibly be?

A burst of laughter draws my attention away from the computer. I've got the TV on too, in case there are any news bulletins that might involve us. I glance over. It's a sitcom—one of those shows where the audience laughs way too much at jokes that aren't that funny. It seems to be about kids in a school on another planet somewhere in outer space.

Suddenly, the camera angle shifts to a close-up of a boy sitting in the back row.

I stare at him in disbelief. It's like I'm looking in a mirror. Okay, maybe not exactly. He's a little bit older. His hair's slightly longer than mine. He seems relaxed and mellow; I haven't been either of those things since learning the truth about Serenity. Other than that, we could be twins.

I peer down at my reflection in the glass cover of the desk. I'm not wrong. This is more than just a passing resemblance. We have the same face.

My mind races. Could I have been cloned from this guy and not Bartholomew Glen? Don't I wish! But it's impossible. This kid would have been a baby when Project Osiris was creating their lab rats. The whole point was to use criminal masterminds, not innocent infants.

No, he must be related to Bartholomew Glen somehow. Which is the same as being related to me.

I watch the show to the end, barely hearing a word of it, yet unable to take my eyes off my mysterious on-screen twin. When the closing credits finally come on, I learn his name: Blake Upton.

Immediately, I swivel back to the computer and Google him.

The picture reminds me of my eighth-grade class photo. I plow through the short biography:

> Blake Upton, 14, is an American actor cur-
> rently appearing as the character Jesse in the
> cable TV sitcom *Jupiter High*, about an Earth
> colony school on the Jovian moon Ganymede.
> The show, which is shooting at Atomic Studios
> in Los Angeles, is the first major role for the
> southern California native . . .

The sound of a door closing draws my attention from the web page. Tori's back. Could she possibly have sold all those cookies? More likely she got sick of dragging the dolly from house to house in the blazing sun.

I'm just about to call to her when I hear voices—two men. I can't make out their exact words, but one of them says something about square footage.

A real estate agent—and he's showing the warehouse to a potential customer!

I mute the TV and press myself up against the door-frame, peering out to see who's there. Two guys in suits are heading my way, moving through the corridor of the office area toward the main warehouse. My first thought is to hide under the desk and hope they don't notice me. Then I remember the car parked beside all those storage shelves. That's going to tip them off.

Out of options, I make a run for the car. I know I'm giving myself away, but that's going to happen anyway. At least now, I've got the element of surprise and a head start.

"Hey, kid—what are you doing here?"

From behind me, the heavy clop of dress shoes accelerates. I'm being chased.

I burst out of the office area, slowing down only to hit

the button on the hanging cable control. The metal loading bay door begins to rattle open.

I jump in the car and waste precious seconds fumbling the keys out of my pocket. By the time I start the engine, both men are in the warehouse, striding toward me.

"Whose car is that? How old are you?" The taller man reaches for the passenger door.

I put the car in gear and step on the gas. That's when I realize my mistake. The rising door is behind me, and in my mad rush, I shifted into Drive. The sedan lurches forward, knocking into a shelf. From high above, a cascade of cookie boxes rains down on the car and the two men.

I finally find Reverse and begin to back up toward the open bay. One of the men reaches the cable box and hits the button. The garage door begins to descend again. I watch it through the rearview mirror, desperately trying to calculate if I've got enough room. It doesn't make any difference, I reflect, because I'm not stopping.

Come on, Eli! I exhort myself. *Faster!*

There's an ear-splitting screech of metal as the bottom of the door scrapes along the roof of the sedan. There's no way the antenna would have made it, but luckily, we cut that off a couple of days ago.

Another screech and I'm free, backing across the

property, heading for the main gate. I've already decided I don't have time to stop and open it. I have to blast right through.

To my surprise, the chain-link barrier offers no resistance and flies open the instant my rear bumper touches it. As I roar out into the road, out of the corner of my eye, I spy a slim figure diving headfirst into the ditch.

I almost hit someone!

I slam on the brakes, and I'm about to jump out and offer assistance when she comes crawling up to the shoulder, rumpled and dusty, but otherwise unhurt.

Tori.

She gets in the passenger seat and buckles her safety belt, just like we were going for a Sunday drive.

"I almost killed you!" I exclaim, shaking.

She shrugs. "It didn't happen. What's up at the warehouse?"

I don't have to answer that question, because at that moment, the two men burst out of the building. One of them is talking into a cell phone.

I floor it and we roar off down the road.

Tori looks worried. "Do you think they got our license plate number?"

I shake my head. "It all happened pretty fast. And

anyway, it wasn't the Purples or anything like that. It was just a real estate guy with a client."

She sighs. "Who would have thought they'd find a new renter so soon? Whoever decorated that place must be color-blind. Everything is beige."

"The cookies probably don't notice." I laugh, which is amazing, since nothing has been funny for a long time. "I'm going to miss the couches, though—a real night's sleep."

"Me too," she agrees. "But the real question is, where do we go from here? All we're doing is running away. We have to make a life for ourselves."

I merge onto a busier road, and slow to the speed of traffic. I'm not such a beginning driver anymore. I'm getting comfortable behind the wheel.

It makes me sad. I've got a perfectly good car, if you discount a few dings on the bumpers and a pretty serious scrape on top of the roof. But I've got no place to go.

Then it dawns on me: yes, I do. I've known it since the minute I first saw him on TV.

"We're going to California—to Atomic Studios." I tell her about Blake Upton, who looks enough like me to be me.

"Do you think he knows anything about Project Osiris?" Tori wonders.

"I doubt it," I admit. "But maybe he can lead us to someone who does."

"I always wanted to go to California," she comments. "They've got some great art museums out there."

"It's a thousand miles away," I put in with a nervous glance at the fuel gauge. "I hope we've got enough gas money."

"No problem." She reaches into her pocket, pulls out a thick wad of cash, and stuffs it into the cup holder between us.

I'm so amazed that I nearly steer off the road into a telephone pole. "Where'd all that money come from?"

She shrugs. "People can't get enough of those Thin Mints."

6

MALIK BRUDER

It's too bad Gus Alabaster is dying, because he's got a really great thing going on. Seriously, when they came up with the expression "living like a boss," I think Gus is the boss they were talking about.

You caught that, right? He said I should call him Gus because it's kind of too late to be calling him Dad. The point is I'm on a first-name basis with the most successful gangster in American history—except that he calls me Bryan. Which *is* a first name; it's just not mine. I'm kind of stuck with that.

The house is awesome. Big deal, there's a lot of fancy gold all over the place. What's wrong with gold? Believe me, when you've got an indoor pool, eighty-inch flat screens in every room, Jacuzzis in the bathrooms, and a full-time chef who cooks whatever you want, whenever you want it, you can put up with a little too much shiny stuff.

The chef part is even better than it sounds, because Gus is too sick to eat anything but soup and Jell-O and oatmeal and things like that. So he told the chef to make whatever *I* want, me being his "son" and all. Do you know there's such a thing as Tater Tots? Back in Happy Valley, they told us we always had the very best, but we didn't have Tater Tots. Another Osiris lie.

Life would be perfect here except for one giant drawback—Laska. What a crab. There's no pleasing that girl. Gus and his people are really nice to us. I mean, we've got our own rooms. We've got new clothes, because Lenny arranged for this swanky store to come over and bring everything in our size, so we could pick what we wanted. Who could find anything wrong with that?

That's easy—Laska.

First she says she doesn't like anything. Then she looks at all the price tags and picks out the cheapest jeans and T-shirts in the pile.

"Come on," I urge. "Why can't you pick out something nice?"

"I don't want anything from these people," she says through clenched teeth. "It's being paid for with dirty money."

"Shhh!" I hiss, inclining my head to indicate Lenny, who's on the other side of the room, talking with the store guy. "You want to get us thrown out of here?"

"We're living off the proceeds of crime," she whispers righteously.

"For thirteen years, we lived off Project Osiris," I point out. "What crime could be worse than that?"

"We *thought* we were living off our families, because they lied to us. In this case, *you're* the one doing the lying. You're letting that awful man go on thinking you're his son. When are you going to tell him the truth? We're never going to find out if he knows anything about Project Osiris until you come clean."

"Shhhhhhhh!!"

"That's the whole reason we're here, isn't it?" she persists. "Not to swim in their pool, and sleep in their beds, and eat their Tater Tots. Who invented those things, anyway? Pure starch and oil!"

"Hey," I shoot back, "you can talk trash about me, but lay off my Tater Tots!"

The reason I'm so mad at her is because she's right.

Not about the Tater Tots, about Gus. I know I have to tell him that I'm not his kid; I'm his clone. But he seems so happy to believe he has a son. The guy's achieved everything imaginable in his career—okay, so his chosen field is crime, but at least he's *good* at it. He's famous. He's rich. He used to hang out with celebrities. The one thing he never got to be was a dad. Until now. And I don't want to spoil it for him.

Sure, some of my reasons are selfish. He's a scary guy, and according to the news articles I've read, he doesn't take kindly to bad news. Also, I'd be admitting that I'm a clone. That could be a pretty big shock to him, especially if he doesn't know much about Project Osiris. Then there's the simple fact that we've got a pretty sweet setup here, so I'd hate to tick him off and get kicked out.

Of course, if he's *really* ticked off, we could get more than just kicked out.

But there's something else too. Gus Alabaster is *me*, or I'm him, or whatever. Yeah, I get it that we're not the same person. But genetically, we are. In a way, he's more than my father. He's my father, mother, and every aunt, uncle, and cousin all rolled into one. If you think about it, no regular person is as closely related to anybody as I am to this dying gangster.

I feel like I have to get to know him if I'm ever going to know myself.

So it's now or never.

"Your girlfriend," Gus says to me. "Not too friendly, is she?"

I stop scratching the soft fur of Counselor's neck. "She's just really shy," I venture with a gulp.

"Bryan—I'm sick; I'm not blind. The girl looks at me like the judge at my sentencing. If she had her way, I'd be back behind bars, dying or not."

I feel a stab of uneasiness. Laska may be a pain in my butt. But with Eli and Tori out of the picture, she's all I've got left. I remember her jumping off that raft to save me from drowning. I've got to stick up for her here.

"She stayed with me all the way from New Mexico, Gus," I remind him.

He nods approvingly. "So she's loyal. That's a plus. Never underestimate that quality. Lot of guys who work for me, they're always smiling—'Hi, Boss. What can I get for you, Boss? You're the man, Boss.' First chance they get, they turn around and stab you in the back. But someone like Lenny—miserable sourpuss, never a smile for anybody, to look at him is to want to punch his lights out—"

"You know I can hear you, right?" comes Lenny's voice from across the room.

Counselor sends a disapproving growl in his direction.

"Smart guy," Gus mutters, grinning. "So there I am, years in the can, no reason to think I'll ever get out. And this mug is running my business, filing appeals, bribing guards to make my life more comfortable. Loyalty."

Lenny saunters over. "I think you should get some rest, Boss. Maybe a little nap."

Gus glares up at him. "Where I'm going, it'll be all nap, all the time. I'm talking to my kid here."

All the other hired guys seem to be really intimidated by Gus. But not Lenny. He's isn't afraid to get into a stare-down with the notorious kingpin. "Dr. Schulman said you should take it easy. And he told *me* to make sure you really do."

"Dr. Schulman is a quack, and he's going to have a hard time digesting that stethoscope when I shove it down his throat."

Lenny casts me a beseeching look, and I stand up. "It's okay, Gus. I'll come back later."

I check on Laska, but when I poke my head inside her room, nobody's there. I'm a little concerned, since she's not exactly popular around here, for obvious reasons. I've got a pet name for the expression on her face basically all the time: the three D's—disapproval, disgust, distrust. The fact that she's not happy here—and doesn't think I should be either—is pretty plain.

Two of the regular guys—Danny and Torque—are in the living room.

"Have you guys seen Amber?"

No response. They're watching a European soccer match on TV and screaming their lungs out over every move, which tells me they've bet a lot of money on this game. That's one thing I've learned about the Alabaster crew—they'll bet on two raindrops running down a windowpane. Even Gus himself, as sick as he is, likes to get in on the action. Although no one wants to bet against Gus, because you have to let him win. No wonder he got so rich.

"Do you know where Amber went?" I repeat, louder this time. "Amber? My—girlfriend?" It isn't getting any easier to call her that.

"Oh, yeah—Amber." Finally, Danny tears his eyes from the screen. "She went out for a run."

It figures. Even when we were hiding at a boarding school in Colorado, psycho Laska had to have her workout. She's too moral to accept all the nice clothes Gus is willing to buy her, but his dirty money is okay to pay for shorts and tank tops so she can keep up her maniac workout routine.

"You know," Torque puts in thoughtfully, "too much exercise is no good for a person. All that perspiration backs up inside your heart. Maybe that's why she's so crabby all the time."

Luckily, I don't have to come up with an answer to this, because Lenny breezes through and reminds the guys to pick up a load of dry cleaning. This sets off a huge argument between Danny and Torque over which one of them has to go. Considering how heated it gets, I can only imagine the kind of money they've got riding on the soccer.

"I'll go," I volunteer.

"Yeah, right," Danny snorts. "It's not around the corner, Bryan. You drive?"

"I drive."

They look dubious, but the idea of staying in front of the game tempts them.

"No fooling?" Torque asks.

"No fooling."

Danny takes out a set of car keys and tosses them to me. "It's the red Benz. Don't screw it up."

When I ask about money or claim checks, Danny shrugs. "Just tell them Lenny sent you. That's all you need." He gives me directions, and they're back in the game like they've forgotten I'm even alive.

Believe it or not, it isn't the nicest car I've ever driven. The one we stole from Tamara Dunleavy was a Bentley, but that's another story.

I find a spot across from the dry cleaner's and enter the store.

The man behind the counter barely looks up from his newspaper. "What can I do for you, kid?"

I follow Danny's instructions, which have brought me this far. "Lenny sent me."

If I told him the building was on fire, I couldn't get a bigger reaction. He leaps up, stands ramrod straight. "Yes, sir! Everything's ready, sir! I'll have it brought out right away!" He races into the back.

Within seconds, a battalion of employees marches up to the front, carrying plastic-wrapped suits and dress shirts. It all looks fine to me, but the guy insists on opening everything up, showing me how "this lapel is pressed exactly according to instructions," and "the crease in these pants was given extra attention."

"I didn't bring any money," I tell him.

"Oh, that's perfectly fine, sir. We'll put it all on Mr. Lenny's tab—with the usual discount, of course." He hesitates. "There was—one slight problem. The tuxedo shirt—there was a stain. We tried our best, and it's mostly gone. See?"

He shows me a snowy sleeve, immaculately starched. There on the cuff is a very faint discoloration. It has a brownish tint now, but I have a feeling it was blood red when it started out—as in real blood.

It's no big deal. If he hadn't told me it was there, I wouldn't have noticed it. But for some reason, I give the guy a hard time. "I don't know if that's going to be okay," I comment.

"Very understandable!" he bleats. "Of course, there will be no charge for that one."

I remain unconvinced. "You know, Lenny can be pretty picky about stuff like this."

He's sweating now. "And naturally, sir, we'll replace the shirt!"

I clam up for a few more seconds just to watch him squirm. I'm not exactly sure why I'm getting such a kick out of this. Maybe I like being called sir. Or it could be the fact that I have all the power, and he has none. I haven't had a racket like this going since Happy Valley, when Hector would do anything for the privilege of being my best friend.

My brow clouds. Hector, who sold us out to Project Osiris, and got Tori and Eli recaptured. Or worse.

"Okay," I tell the guy, who looks like he's almost ready to faint. "Don't worry about it."

They insist on bringing the stuff out to the car for me and load it in like it's delicate crystal instead of a bunch of clothes. Then every single employee apologizes for the stain and thanks me for being so understanding. As I drive away from there, it's like I'm ten feet tall. I can't help thinking: Gus must feel this way every minute of his life. What could be better than having people falling over themselves to please you? I'll bet even in prison, he had the best of everything. How awesome is that?

By the time I get back to the house, the soccer game is over. Danny is sprawled out on the couch with a wet towel covering his face. Torque, on the other hand, wears a cake-eating grin, as he counts out a wad of bills that would choke a hippo.

I drape the dry cleaning over a loveseat.

"Thanks, kid." He peels a crisp hundred off the roll and slaps it into my hand.

I could get used to this.

7

ELI FRIEDEN

Twenty-three hours feels like a lifetime when you're scared out of your mind.

That's how long it takes us to drive from Amarillo to Burbank, California, where Blake Upton's TV show, *Jupiter High*, is in production.

There are so many things that can go wrong. What if our car has been reported stolen? What if somebody notices that I look too young to drive? Every time we pass a police cruiser, we both hold our breath and try to act casual. Twenty miles in, my shoulders ache from trying to sit taller behind the wheel.

We make it out of Amarillo okay, but then we cross into New Mexico, which brings up all kinds of weird memories. We're well south of Serenity—which we know is empty anyway. But I can tell that Tori is thinking about her parents. I'm thinking about my father too, even though Felix Frieden—Felix *Hammerstrom*—is the mad scientist behind Project Osiris. If the whole experiment is sick, then he's the head sicko. And even so, I miss him. I suppose what I really miss is having a family, a home, a place I belong.

We stop on the outskirts of Albuquerque and grab dinner at a crowded Taco Bell. I wanted to stop somewhere more out of the way, but Tori insists that we're better off where there are a lot of people around.

"A couple of kids are going to stand out if they're the only customers at some roadside diner in a town where everybody knows everybody else," she explains. "Here, we can blend in."

Tori's pretty smart when it comes to things like this. Either that, or it's Yvonne-Marie Delacroix and her instincts for living on the lam.

We gas up and get back in the car, determined to push straight through to California. It's rough. We're driving on the same interstate through total darkness all night. We polish off the rest of New Mexico, cross the entire state of Arizona, and enter California surrounded by mind-numbing black. By three in the morning, I'm slapping myself in the face just to keep from dropping off. Tori pledges to keep me awake and alert with conversation, and promptly falls asleep. She even has the nerve to snore. I've never been so jealous of anyone in my life.

I have no idea how I make it. It's almost like my head isn't attached to my body anymore and is floating a few feet above me like a helium balloon.

The gas holds out until Needles, California, in the middle of the Mojave Desert. It's dawn, and I'm surrounded by tumbleweeds, cactus, and scrub. I expect a bit of a chill in the air, like Serenity in the early morning. But it's already baking hot. The mere act of filling the car leaves me bathed in sweat.

Tori wakes up and buys every caffeinated drink at the mini-mart. But when we get back to the air-conditioning of the car, all we want is the big jug of water.

We reach Los Angeles a little before noon, and stop at a gas station to buy a city map. If we hadn't wrecked the car's GPS, finding Atomic Studios would be easy. But it's too late to undo that now. Worse, LA isn't the same as other cities. It goes on forever in all directions, and most of it is crammed with traffic. It still takes hours to inch along the jammed highways to Burbank.

To our surprise, Atomic Studios isn't just a building. It's more like an entire town, surrounded by high walls and a security gate. On the sprawling campus, we can see several huge warehouse-like structures and entire neighborhoods of small bungalows. Cars and golf carts zip around a complex system of roadways.

"It's bigger than Serenity!" I exclaim from my vantage point atop a boulder, peering over the boundary wall.

Tori joins me on the rock. "And it's so tastefully landscaped. I love the color contrast they've created using lush green tropical plants against the desert browns and beiges of the native landscape."

"I'm not planning to paint a picture of it," I tell her, a little crankily, due to lack of sleep. "What we need is a way to get past that gate."

We watch as cars arrive and pull up to the gatehouse. A guard emerges, peers into every vehicle, and checks photo IDs. Security is tight. Names are checked against a list of visitors on a clipboard. On top of that, a second guard inside the glass booth phones ahead to make sure the newcomer is expected.

"You're a good liar," I praise Tori. "You think you could bluff our way through there?"

She shakes her head sadly. "Even if I could come up with the right story, they're checking IDs. Neither of us has that."

"Can we find a secluded spot and climb the wall?" I suggest.

She points to the top of the tall fencing. "Cameras. At regular intervals all the way around. There might even be pressure sensors that go off if anyone tries to get over."

I'm mystified. "What is this place, Fort Knox? Why do they need so much security? All they do here is make TV shows."

Tori thinks it over. "In Serenity, no one was more famous than anybody else, because we all knew each other. But if you're famous in the outside world—like a TV star, for instance—millions of people know you. And how are you supposed to live your life if you've got a big crowd mobbing you all the time?"

"Well, that's just great!" I snap. Tori's only crime is being right, but all my frustration bubbles over at her. I've just driven over a thousand miles; I've been up nonstop for a day and a half, all so I can see one guy. "How am I supposed to meet Blake Upton if I can't even get past the gate?"

And then a voice from below calls, "Blake?"

We look down. A golf cart with a flashing light on the roof and *STUDIO SECURITY* stenciled on the side has pulled onto the shoulder of the road. A uniformed guard is peering up at us.

"Blake?" she repeats. "Is that you?"

I manage a slight wave. "Uh—hi."

"What are you doing up there?" she demands. "You were supposed to be in makeup twenty minutes ago."

Blake. She called me Blake. *She thinks I'm him.*

I noticed the close resemblance back in the cookie warehouse, but it never occurred to me that I could pass for the guy. This is my way in!

I hesitate. Do I dare? Sooner or later, someone is going to realize I'm not Blake Upton. If no one else, Blake Upton himself is going to know. What if he has me thrown out before I get a chance to ask him some questions—like why are we nearly identical?

I'm frozen on the boulder. I'd give anything for Tori's advice, but I can't start a big conversation about it right in front of the security lady.

I shoot Tori a pleading glance, begging for an answer she can't give me.

She hisses, "You're showing me where you work," and shoves me off the rock.

It's so unexpected that I'm relaxed, and the fall doesn't kill me. I land on both feet and manage to stay upright. "This is my friend Tori. I'm showing her the studio."

I'm right next to the golf cart. The security lady can see

me just fine, and she doesn't denounce me as an imposter.

"Hop on," she invites. "I'll give you a ride."

That's how we not only get in past the gate, but are chauffeured directly to the soundstage where *Jupiter High* is being filmed.

We pause at the entrance. "I've always wanted to see how a real TV show gets made," Tori confides.

I'm so scared that I can hardly put one foot in front of the other, and she's going all tourist on me.

After the bright sunshine outdoors, the studio itself seems dark. A tall, skinny guy in a headset, carrying a clipboard, hurries toward us, gesturing to a light-up sign that reads *QUIET.* At the center of the gloom is a brilliantly lit stage made up to look like a classroom. A scene is underway, and we can hear the actors' voices as well as laughter from a small studio audience.

When the clipboard guy gets a good look at me, he does a double take. He leans right in to my ear and barely whispers, "Are you his brother?"

There's no answer for that. A clone can't be anybody's brother. So I just follow the *QUIET* instruction.

Eventually, the *Jupiter High* scene ends and the lights come on all around us. Tori claps along with the studio audience. I look for Clipboard, but he's nowhere to be found.

A moment later, he reappears with Blake Upton in tow.

Tori squeezes my arm and mouths these words: *He's gorgeous!*

Gorgeous? What's that supposed to mean? The guy looks like *me*.

The young actor is saying, "But I don't have a brother—"

Then he sees me. Our eyes lock. His are getting wider by the minute.

Okay, we're not exactly alike. He's older than me and a little taller. His shoulders are broader, and his cheeks are fuller. That's probably because I've been on the run, living on Girl Scout Cookies and Mountain Dew. But we have the same face.

"Who *are* you?" he asks in a disbelieving voice.

Considering I've planned this entire conversation, I can barely stammer out the words. "My name is Eli Frieden. I come from a small town in New Mexico. And the minute I saw you on TV, I knew we had to be related."

"Related?" Clipboard echoes. "You're practically twins!"

Blake looks even more bewildered. "So you came to California to find me? Why didn't you just ask your parents?"

"My parents are dead," I lie, laying out the story I crafted to avoid having to admit the clone thing. "I'm adopted. The only thing they told me about my biological parents is that they were related to a man named Bartholomew Glen."

"Glen?" Clipboard blurts. "You mean the murderer? The Crossword Killer?"

"Wait a minute," Blake exclaims. "If I'm related to you, and you're related to him, that means—*I'm* related to Bartholomew Glen?"

"I admit it sounds bad when you put it that way—" I begin.

"You're crazy! Don't you think I'd know if there was someone like that in my family? Don't you think my parents would?"

The clipboard guy tries to calm him down. "Blake, take it easy. You don't want to strain your voice in the middle of a shoot."

"But, Kenny, don't you see what this kid's trying to pull? He looks like me, so he cooks up some cockamamie story about the Crossword Killer so he can blackmail me!"

Tori steps forward. "Eli doesn't want your money; he wants your help. He's just trying to find his roots."

"By saying I'm related to the worst person in history?" Blake shoots back.

I try to reason with him. "Just because you have bad

DNA doesn't mean you're bad. Trust me, I've thought about this a lot."

"I don't have any bad DNA, and neither do you! You're making all this up to get something out of me! Well, it won't work—"

A balding middle-aged man pushes his way into our group. "All right, Blake, you're holding up the works. Why are you sweating?" He turns away. "Can I get some makeup over here?" Then he sees me.

He looks from Blake to me and back to the young actor. "Somebody want to let the director in on what's the story here?"

"No story, Amos," Blake says angrily. "This kid looks like me. But that's all. He's trying to say we're cousins or something."

"You think we're not?" I demand, showing more confidence than I feel.

The director examines me like I'm a specimen on a microscope slide. "He's the spitting image of you, Blake."

I make my appeal to the director. "I'm not trying to scam him. I'm just trying to find out if we're both related to the same person."

"Bartholomew Glen," Clipboard supplies.

Amos stares at me. "Kid, you should seek professional help."

I play my last card. "I'm willing to take a DNA test."

"We don't do those here," the director explains. "We make TV shows. You upset my actor, you upset me. Get off my set. Kenny, have security escort these two off the lot."

Kenny leads us outside. "The golf cart will pick you up here." He smiles sympathetically. "For what it's worth, I think you must be related. But the Crossword Killer—that part's too weird."

The door closes behind us and we're outside. I come to a stop. Tori keeps on walking.

"Where are you going? They said wait here."

She wheels around, grabs my arm, and starts pulling me. "It was pure luck that we made it through that gate at all. If we let ourselves get kicked out, we'll never get back in—not when every guard in this place has been told to be on the alert for a kid who looks exactly like Blake Upton."

"Yeah, but Blake's not going to help us anyway, so what's the point of us being here?"

"He'll help us," she promises.

"Are you nuts? He's why we got the boot!"

"Because you're in his head," she reasons, picking up

the pace as we turn a corner and start down a narrow street with small, neat bungalows on either side. "He knows you're too much alike for it to be a coincidence. You'll wear him down. Trust me."

"So you want to hide out *here*?" I counter. "How's that even possible? They've got security golf carts patrolling the whole place. You think they won't notice two kids sleeping in the cactus garden?"

"Look at these little houses." Her sweeping gesture takes in the neighborhood of bungalows. "See how they've got names on the doors? They must be for people who come here to work on movies and TV shows. But every so often you come to one that has no name. The blinds are drawn. The place is dark. This one, for instance. Check it out."

The small cottage is virtually identical to all the others, white stucco with a red-tile roof. This one's at the end of a cul-de-sac, out of sight of the main road. You can detect the slightly darker spot on the door, where the nameplate would hang.

I'm about to say "maybe the sign fell off" when Tori marches up the short walk and rings the bell. I rush up to stand beside her. Solidarity, I guess. It's not like there's much either of us can do if she's wrong and somebody answers that door.

Nobody does. There's not a sound coming from inside the small structure.

Tori flashes me a triumphant grin. "You see?"

"This could be the place they're going to give to the next new guy," I warn.

She seems exasperated. "And maybe the moon will fall out of the sky. We'll deal with that when it happens. For now, we're moving in."

We circle the bungalow, and Tori checks the windows. They're all locked.

"Now what?" I ask. "Try another house?"

She shoots me a sweet smile, picks up a baseball-size rock from the cactus garden, and punches through the back window. It's such a surgical strike that it leaves only a neat round hole in the corner of the glass. Then she carefully inserts her arm, reaches up to the sash, and flips the latch. We raise the window and climb inside.

"What if someone notices the broken window?" I ask.

"Who's going to notice?" She points outside, where a palm grove begins not ten feet from the back. "The coconuts?" She sits down on the couch and leans back with a dreamy expression. "Blake Upton. Wow!"

For some reason, that irritates me. "Before yesterday, you never even heard of the guy."

"Another thing I missed by growing up in Serenity." She repeats that really annoying "Wow!"

"He's not there for your viewing pleasure," I remind her. "We need serious information from the guy."

"Oh, we'll get that," she replies determinedly. "A pretty face isn't going to stand in our way."

8

AMBER LASKA

When we first found out what Project Osiris was and the kind of people we were cloned from, the big question was this: Are we them or are we us? Yeah, we match them physically, but are we the same people? They're so awful that even the idea of being a little bit like them is really disturbing.

Now, finally, we have our answer, and it's definitely *not* what I wanted to hear. We're them, all right. Or at least Malik is. He's turning into a gangster.

Ever since Danny and Torque gave him a hundred bucks after he brought back their stupid dry cleaning, he's turned into the errand boy for the entire Alabaster organization. Now every goon in Chicago who's too lazy to put gas in his car, pick up the Chinese food, or buy his mom a birthday present is paying Malik to do it for him. The slogan around the house is "Leave it to Bryan"—Bryan being Malik.

"They're using you!" I plead. "They're treating you like their personal slave!"

In answer, Malik pulls a fat wad of bills out of his pocket and flips through it like it's a deck of cards. Fifties and hundreds.

"Money!" I exclaim. "Is that all that matters to you?"

He gives that shrug that rubs me the wrong way and says, "I'll let you know if I think of anything else I care about."

"We're supposed to care about making a life for ourselves," I remind him. "We're the only ones free, you know. And how about the clones who are still in the hands of Osiris? Who's going to get justice for them if not us?"

He looks a little sheepish but still defiant. "That's what we're here for—to see what Gus knows about Project Osiris."

"Yeah, and how's that going?" I challenge. "He still thinks you're his son. You haven't even told him who you really are yet!"

"I'm just waiting for the right moment," he insists. "He's so happy he's got a kid. He's even proud of me. No one's ever been proud of me before."

"What's to be proud of? That you can pick up a few suits without dropping them down the sewer?"

He's insulted. "I'm not just a gofer. I do other things too. This morning, I picked up a package from this guy with three fingers, and Cyrus gave me two hundred bucks."

"It was probably a gun," I growl. "Or worse, the missing fingers. Malik, we can't stay here much longer—"

"Shhh! I'm Bryan."

"Don't you get it? This is *wrong*," I insist. "You're becoming exactly what Project Osiris was invented to see if we'd turn into!"

"That's not true!"

"Isn't it? We're living with criminals, letting them feed us and buy us clothes. And now you're working for them, earning big tips. Who knows what was in that package! For sure something that could get you arrested."

He reddens. "So maybe I am turning into Gus! So what? Would that be so terrible? He's rich; he's smart; he's got dozens of guys who do whatever he tells them! And you know what? I like him! And he likes me too! You're just jealous because you don't have anybody like that!"

It stings—and not because I'm yearning to find Mickey Seven in prison in Florida and pretend we're family. Mickey Seven is a terrorist, and I hate her for that. In fact, the things she did fill me with so much hate that I can imagine myself turning into her or someone like her. And that scares the life out of me.

I storm out of there to avoid a bigger argument. Back in my room, I find my latest to-do list, only half-finished. When I see it, I experience a wave of shame. It's mainly about exercising and eating healthy. Gus's chef is so happy to be making something besides Tater Tots that he keeps coming up with the most fantastic salads and steamed vegetable dishes for me. Suddenly, I feel really shallow.

I cross it all out and pencil in a single item:

THINGS TO DO TODAY
- Something positive!

If we're stuck here, and Malik insists on living the gangster life, then I'm going to counteract that by being good.

"Sure thing, Toots," Danny tells me when I ask him for a lift. "Hop in the car."

I give him the address that I got off the internet.

He frowns. "That's not a very nice neighborhood. You sure you want to go there?"

"I've never been surer of anything in my life."

We get in the car and he loops around the circular driveway. "What is this place, anyway?"

"You let me worry about that."

As we drive, our surroundings get seedier and more run-down. I've seen a lot of tough neighborhoods since leaving Serenity, but Chicago takes the prize. The area is not just poor. It's also old. Everything looks like it's in the process of crumbling. I'd never admit it to Danny—and definitely not to Malik—but I'm feeling pretty nervous.

We pull up in front of the one building in several blocks that has a reasonably fresh coat of paint on the woodwork. The sign in the flyspecked window reads:

NEW HOPE
SOUP KITCHEN

Danny puts up the top of his convertible and turns to face me. "We got the wrong address," he says.

"No, this is the place," I inform him cheerfully. "I work here."

"Doing what?"

"I volunteer." To be honest, I have no idea what my job will be. But the guy on the phone said they definitely need volunteers, so here I am.

"Listen, Amber—" Danny's really frazzled now. "I can't leave you here. Bryan wouldn't like it. And worse, he might tell Gus!"

"Bryan's not my boss. And neither is Gus."

He winces. "Don't say that. Somebody might hear you."

I jump out of the car. "Thanks for the ride. I'll take the bus home."

I go in and they put me right to work. And work means work. Even in Serenity, when I was the good girl, the teacher's daughter, who tried three times harder than everybody else, I never understood the real meaning of the word. I start off filling huge industrial dishwashers in a room so full of steam that you can barely see your hand in front of your face. My hair is standing straight out around my head, my blond roots exposed to the world.

All that lifting and bending and loading is pretty back-breaking. So I'm relieved when I graduate to slicing carrots for the soup. That's being made in a vat big enough for a water buffalo to take a bath in. Now just my wrist is sore, instead of my entire body. But just when I'm getting good with the big knife, the dinner rush hits full swing, and they need me to help serve.

That's when I get my first look at the New Hope

Soup Kitchen going full speed. The long cafeteria-style tables are packed with diners, mostly men. I expected a rowdier scene, but the place is nearly silent, except for the clink of cutlery. These are hungry people, and eating is serious business. The food line stretches out the door and wraps around the side of the building. My job is ladling out baked beans, one scoop per tray—*slop!*—and on to the next person.

The quiet feels so unnatural that I start talking: "Best beans in the city . . . Enjoy your dinner . . . Careful, they're hot . . . Satisfaction guaranteed."

I start to get answers. People say thank you. They smile. They even find a few words to say to each other. I feel good, like maybe I had something to do with warming up the room, making a *difference*. It's funny—in Serenity, our parents were always telling us about helping one another. But we never actually had to do it, because the place was phony and nobody really needed any help. I get it now, though. I finally get it.

The place is a madhouse for about an hour and a half before things quiet down a little. We're still serving, but there's no more line, and people have stopped arriving.

That's why I look up when the door opens, the bell on

the knob announcing a new arrival. This one's not looking for dinner; he's looking for me.

Malik.

I peer past him and spot the convertible double-parked at the curb, Danny at the wheel and Torque in the passenger seat. Their expressions are alert, like they might have to fight their way out of this neighborhood. Pretty wimpy for a couple of mob guys. I've just fed half the zip code, handing out friendliness with my baked beans, and getting nothing but the same in return.

Malik walks right up to the counter. "We're leaving."

I glare at him. "*You're* leaving. I'm not done yet."

He starts to walk behind the steam trays, but the manager stops him. "You're not allowed back here without a hairnet."

Malik's face is pure Gus Alabaster. "I'm not putting on any hairnet!" But he advances no farther.

I set down my ladle and come out to confront him. "What do you want, Malik?"

"Look," he tells me. "The guys are right outside in the car. You've made your point. Now it's time to go."

I fold my arms across my bean-spattered apron. "And what point is that exactly?"

"I don't know," he complains. "You have to be a genius

to figure out why you do the things you do! I only said it because maybe there's a reason besides the fact that you're nuts!"

I lower my voice. "You're getting more like these gangsters every day. So I came here to do some good to balance out all your bad."

He stares at me. "Not another person on earth thinks the way you do. Except maybe Mickey Seven, and she used to blow up buildings."

"Look who's talking!" I retort. "You're going to get yourself arrested and flush everything we're trying to do down the toilet!"

"Give me a break!" he barks at top volume. "If it wasn't for me, you'd be sleeping in the street! I ought to—"

A big guy, pretty tattered, pushes back his chair and interposes his bulk between Malik and me. I think I might have given him an extra half scoop of beans because he seemed really hungry.

"This guy bothering you, sweetheart?"

I'm really tempted to say yes. But Danny and Torque are out of the car and have their faces pressed to the window. If they decide that their boss's "son" is in danger, things are going to get ugly.

A few of the other diners are noticing too.

"Leave her alone, kid," someone calls. "She's nice."

"Quit hassling the bean lady."

"If you didn't come to eat, get out of here."

"It's fine, you guys," I say hastily. To Malik, I whisper. "Please leave before there's trouble. I'll take the bus home."

"We'll wait for you. Hurry up."

I'm basically done, but I hang around for another half hour, just to make him sweat. I see him through the window, doing a slow burn. Good.

When I get to the car, Torque asks me, "How was work, honey?" And the two gangsters crack up laughing.

Malik doesn't think it's very funny.

At the Alabaster house, Danny wanders off. Malik and I are about to follow him inside when Torque calls us back to the car.

"Let me give you kids a piece of advice," he drawls, his expression unreadable. "You talk too loud."

Malik is one of the guys now, so he just laughs. But I can tell he's worried about where Torque might be going with this.

"You think?" I ask, working to keep my voice steady.

Torque nods lazily. He has these droopy eyelids, so he always seems half-asleep. But the eyes behind them are laser sharp. "Especially around the house. You never know who might be listening."

"What did you hear?" I rasp.

"Not much," he replies airily. "Just that you two aren't who you say you are. And that Bryan here isn't really Gus's kid."

We've gotten a lot of nasty shocks since discovering the truth about ourselves and Project Osiris. It's interesting that, no matter how steadily the bad news keeps on coming, you never get used to it. Malik and I exchange a look of pure terror.

"So," Torque goes on conversationally, "my question is this: If you're not the boss's son, who are you?"

9

TORI PRITEL

So this is Hollywood.

We didn't learn much about the outside world in Serenity, but they let us have movies and TV. Not the violent stuff, obviously. We weren't exposed to anything about war or crime or fighting. Still, one of the few things we had in common with the other kids on the planet was that we knew there was a place called Hollywood where all this entertainment came from.

And now Eli and I are right in the heart of it—Bungalow 149, Atomic Studios, Burbank, California. The bungalows are mostly used as offices and crash pads for writers and directors working on projects here. And now two fugitive clones. But we're the only ones who know about that.

Eli and I lie low at first, which is what Yvonne-Marie Delacroix would probably do. We keep to our hideout, steering clear of the windows for fear of being spotted by studio security. Eventually, though, I have to venture out in search of food. There's no grocery store, but the studio commissary is huge, and the food is fantastic. Better still, you see actors eating there—the famous and the beautiful (think: Blake Upton!!!). The less successful ones are kind of fun too. You play a game with yourself: What TV show do I know that guy from? Wasn't she in something I've seen?

The only bummer is that Eli can't share this with me. Security could be searching for a Blake look-alike. So I bring food back to him.

"Will Ferrell was sitting two tables away from me," I tell Eli, handing him a shrink-wrapped sandwich. "He was having chicken à la king."

He takes an unenthusiastic bite. "You know how much I care about what Will Ferrell is having for dinner? About as much as I cared about that guy from *The Big Bang Theory* having a burrito for lunch."

"*Vegetarian* burrito," I amend.

"Tori, you're killing me," Eli groans. "I can't stand

being cooped up here. And for what? Blake Upton is never going to listen to us."

"Sure, he is," I assure him. "He was in the commissary too. He was checking me out all through dinner."

He's alarmed. "He recognized you?"

"Of course he recognized me. And he didn't call security either."

Eli's eyes narrow. "He didn't talk to you, did he?"

"Don't I wish! No, he was on the other side of the room."

"Because I thought maybe he invited you to his high school prom," he says sulkily. "And we have to put everything we're doing on hold while you go dress shopping."

I stare at him. He's *jealous*! Of Blake Upton—who looks so much like him that they could be twins! If our situation wasn't so awful, I'd laugh in his face.

"There's no dress shopping and no prom. He recognizes *me* because he's thinking about *you*. I told you—you're in his head."

"We can't wait around for some actor." Eli points to the computer on the desk. "I was online today, researching Bartholomew Glen. You know where he is right now? Noranda State Penitentiary, about seventy miles north of here. We could pick up the car and be there in barely an hour."

"But if that turns out to be a dead end, we'll never get back on studio property," I reason. "We've got to be patient and take one more crack at Blake. Trust me."

"I looked Blake up too," Eli informs me. "I think *Jupiter High* is his first big show, because there isn't a lot about him. But he has over five hundred thousand followers on Twitter."

"Twitter? What's that?"

He takes me to the computer and shows me a web page with an endless procession of thumbnail photographs. They're all kids, mostly girls (duh), wearing Blake T-shirts, and hugging Blake posters. They're accompanied by short messages: *You're the best, Blake . . . #1 Actor . . . Blake for president . . . I love you, Blake . . .*

As we watch, new postings pop up constantly. "Wow," I breathe.

"Stop saying that!" he snaps in annoyance.

"These kids worship him!"

"That must be because he's so *gorgeous*," Eli puts in sarcastically.

I ignore that crack. "The occasional one says he's a jerk, but most are big fans."

"And every now and then, Mr. Wonderful himself posts

an answer. See?" Eli scrolls up to a tweet next to a picture of the actor's handsome face:

> Thanks guys! Glad you enjoy the show! #BestFansEver.

"That means he reads this!" I conclude.

"Some of it, anyway. If you're famous, you want to know what people think of you." He looks up at me. "So what?"

An idea is taking shape in my mind. "If you're sick of being stuck in the house," I tell him, "tomorrow's your lucky day."

When Eli steps into the sun the next morning, he squints like a mole coming out of a burrow. I spent an hour and a half trimming his hair and blow-drying it, and now he's Blake Upton 100 percent. I defy Blake's own mother to tell them apart. Amber never agreed with me when I said Eli was really good-looking, but here's the proof. He's a dead ringer for a TV star with more than half a million Twitter followers.

It's at least a mile across the Atomic property to the main gate. The first time one of the golf carts drives by, Eli practically jumps out of his skin. That's how nervous he is.

We pass soundstages and the commissary, and arrive

just in time to see the crowd gathering for the studio tour—which is a big deal at Atomic. Dozens of people are lined up behind velvet ropes waiting for the open-air bus.

"All right, 'Blake,'" I whisper to Eli. "Do your stuff."

"I'm really not sure what I'm supposed to—"

Well, I wasn't cloned from some quiet hermit who didn't know how to make things happen. I cup my hands to my mouth and squeal at the top of my lungs, *"Oh, my God! It's him! Blake Upton!"*

A chorus of answering screams cut the air.

A girl of ten or eleven vaults the rope and makes a bull run at Eli, shrieking all the way. "You're my favorite actor! Wait till I tell everybody I know . . . !"

That's all it takes. Pretty soon, Eli is mobbed by an adoring crowd. Cell phone cameras begin clicking. He's signing autographs.

Oh, please, I think, *let him remember to write Blake's name and not his own.*

When the tour bus pulls up, only a few people are still in line. The rest are gathered in the worshipful throng around Eli.

That's when a familiar figure steps out of the commissary and climbs into a golf cart. It's the *Jupiter High* director, Amos. I feel a stab of fear. When that cart loops around to head for the soundstage, Amos is going to see "Blake" signing autographs and posing for selfies. What if he just left Blake at breakfast, or took a phone call from him that he's stuck in traffic? (I'd bet my life on their resemblance, but nobody can be in two places at once.)

The golf cart is getting closer. In a few seconds, Eli will be in full view.

I sprint for the crowd, blast through to the center, and dive at Eli's knees. He folds up like a deck chair, crumpling to the ground beside me. His expression is pure shock.

"Oh, Blake," I holler at him. "Sign my forehead!"

He looks at me like I've lost my mind.

By the time we struggle to our feet, the golf cart is heading away, Amos's back to us.

As the girl who wiped out their idol, I'm not too popular among the Blake Upton fans. I get a little rough treatment until the tour guide comes over and hustles his passengers onto the studio bus.

"What was that for?" Eli demands, limping a little as we start away.

"Keep your head down," I mumble. "Amos almost saw you, but I think the coast is clear."

We make our way back to Bungalow 149 and pounce on the computer. It's happening already. Blake's Twitter feed is going crazy with the people from the studio tour. Their bus can be scarcely half a block from the main gate, and they're already tweeting their pictures and selfies with Eli: *Me with Blake Upton at Atomic Studios . . . BU OMG!! #EvenHotterInPerson . . . He's so nice! . . . BU signed my arm! #NeverWashAgain . . .*

There's even a picture of Eli with me that must have been taken from the bus. The message reads: *Blake's girlfriend??? #HeCanDoBetter.*

(I don't know whether to laugh or be insulted.)

"How do we know Blake's even going to see this stuff?" Eli asks uncertainly.

"He'll see it," I assure him. "And if he doesn't, someone's bound to tell him about it."

I make sure I'm in the commissary when Blake's cast and crew break for lunch. As always, he eats with one eye on his phone. Then he puts down his sandwich, and both eyes are on the small screen.

He glances my way, which makes my heart jump a little. I shoot him my most dazzling smile, and he returns to the phone, pale and haunted.

I experience an unexpected pang of sympathy for the guy. It can't be fun to see pictures of yourself doing things you know you never did.

I go up to the dessert table to get some rhubarb pie. Chris Hemsworth had this yesterday, and he really seemed to enjoy it. I feel a tap on my shoulder, and turn around to come face-to-face with Blake.

It's the first time I've ever been this close to him. I should be quaking in my sneakers but I'm totally in control. Maybe Yvonne-Marie Delacroix has an internal switch that keeps her all business when a plan is under way. I obviously have one too.

"I hear the rhubarb pie is good," I tell him in a friendly tone.

He's obviously shaken. "Forget the pie. We need to talk."

10

MALIK BRUDER

Consequences. That's the word Torque uses.

There are consequences when you lie to Gus Alabaster, and tell him you're his son when you're not. There are consequences when you don't watch what you say, and someone like Torque finds out you're lying. And there are definitely consequences when the Torques of the world realize that they have something on you.

Now he's got me doing his dirty work, and it has nothing to do with picking up dry cleaning or Chinese food. I've taken over his whole job while he sits around playing cards or watching sports on TV. And the great tips I was getting before for doing next to nothing? Forget that. Now I'm working for free. If I dare to complain about that, Torque tells me that, by all rights, he should be charging me hush money to remain silent about what he knows.

"You're a nice kid, but you've got a thing or two to learn about how it works," he lectures me. "I'm keeping a pretty big secret for you. So how it works is you do what I say, and you like it. No—you love it."

I don't love it. There's nothing to love. Basically, I pick up envelopes of money from these store owners who pay us for "protection." The thing is, it's really protection from *us*, because if they don't pay, we make sure something bad happens to their business. Remember that first time at the dry cleaner's, when the owner was so scared, and it made me feel like a big man? I don't feel that way anymore. When I walk into one of those stores, they're not just scared of me; they hate my guts. When they hand over the envelope, they wish it would explode in my face. And the worst part is I don't blame them. How would you feel if you built up a business only to have some guy squeeze you for cash every week not to set fire to it, or heave a brick through the window? I'd hate me too.

That's one way I'm different from Gus. He doesn't seem to have a problem with being despised, but I can't stand it. I'm not sure why that is, since we have the same DNA. Maybe it's this: when I was growing up in Serenity, I always believed my parents loved me. It was a lie, of course.

They were scientists; I was their experiment. But once you feel what it is to be loved, it's pretty hard to have people look at you with loathing.

Gus seems so cool because he has yachts and private jets and houses all over the place. You never really consider that the money to pay for all that comes from having a guy like Torque going door to door, threatening people.

And now, a guy like me.

What makes it even harder to accept is that Gus and I have gotten kind of close. He's proud of the fact that his "son" gets along with his crew. Even though he's becoming so weak that he can't really hold a conversation for very long, he makes sure that I go in to see him at least a couple of times every day. He talks about the future, maybe one day sending me to college. That's a big deal, because college is super-expensive, and Gus—rich as he is—is famous for being tight fisted with his cash.

I catch a sad shake of the head from Lenny. Gus doesn't have a future.

Sometimes he's not strong enough to talk, but he calls me in anyway, just to stare at me.

"Can you believe it, Counselor?" he mumbles to the dog. "It's like I'm looking in the mirror forty-five years ago."

I have to tell him the truth. He's given me the perfect opening. *Yeah, Gus, it should be like looking in the mirror, because I'm not your son; I'm you.*

He should know. He deserves to know. And *I* deserve to get Torque off my back. The guy can't very well blackmail me over a secret that's not a secret anymore.

I can't do it. There's no way to tell if Gus is even alert enough to process that kind of crazy information. Or worse, he might think I'm lying to him, betraying him. And yeah, I'm a little bit scared. People who betray Gus tend to end up at the bottom of Lake Michigan. But mostly, I don't want to spoil the good feeling he gets out of thinking he has a son. The doctors say he hasn't got much time left.

"You didn't tell him?" Amber's eyes bulge. "Malik, what were you thinking?"

"Shhh!" I hiss. "The last time you shot your mouth off you brought Torque down on my neck!"

She lowers her sound level but her nagging level is still full power. "How could you miss an opportunity like that? You may never get another one! What are you waiting for? Until he's so weak that he can't even talk? Then how much information are we going to get out of him?"

"We can't even be sure he knows anything at all," I mumble.

"We'll never find out unless we ask! That was the whole point of coming to Chicago in the first place! Not so you could take the gangster lifestyle out for a test-drive!"

"You take that back!" I spit at her. "The gangster lifestyle stinks, but at least I'm not slinging beans at people who don't know what soap is!"

Her anger is so great that her nostrils flare, but her voice is deathly quiet. "Those people are my friends. I don't know how they ended up in a soup kitchen. Chances are, some of them messed up; the rest were just unlucky. A few of them talk to themselves and see things that aren't there. But you know what? They need me, and I've been able to add something to their lives besides a free meal. They like me, and I like them." She adds, "Better than I like you."

I stare at her. She's mad at me, and I'm mad at her. It should be a fair fight, but it isn't. Because I'm never going to get as riled up as Laska.

The place is a hole-in-the-wall stationery and card shop that also carries small gifts and dumb souvenirs of Chicago attractions. At this point, I don't even notice what the stores do anymore. I don't care if they're repairing shoes or flipping burgers or selling cocker spaniels. It's all the same to me.

The girl at the counter is not much older than I am, and really cute. It might be nice to talk to her, except I know that as soon as she finds out what I'm here for, she's going to clam up and shrink away like I've got Ebola. So I just mutter, "I need to talk to the owner."

She gets him out of the back—middle-aged, balding, kind of on the short side, another boring nice guy whose day I'm about to ruin.

"What can I do for you, son?"

I say the three words that I dread almost as much as he will. "Torque sent me."

He goes white to the ears, but it's clear he's been expecting Torque or someone like him. With a key, he unlocks a drawer and pulls out an envelope. I'm just noticing that it looks kind of thin, when he offers, in a trembling voice, "It's a little light this week."

"Torque's not going to like that," I reply automatically.

He's starting to sweat. "Business has been slow. All those free e-cards on the internet. And my wife needs her gallbladder taken out. Insurance barely covers half . . ." His voice trails off.

I know exactly what I'm supposed to say. Torque gave me the whole script. I'm supposed to look at the most expensive thing in the store—in this dump, it's probably the plate-glass window in front. And my line is: *Nice window you got here, pal. It would be a real shame if somebody put a brick through it.* And he'd get the message that, as bad as things may be, they could get a whole lot worse if he doesn't pay.

I open my mouth to say it, and what comes out surprises even me. "Please, mister. Just pay. If you don't, he'll mess up your store and maybe you too. And he won't let you out of one cent of what you owe!"

The guy's almost in tears. "I haven't got it. My wife's doctor bills—I'd pay if I could, but you can't get blood out of a stone."

I reach into my pocket and pull out a wad of bills. "Look, this is all I got. You can have it. Fifty—seventy—seventy-three bucks. Is that enough?"

He stares at me like I've gone insane. I probably have. On some level, I understand that I can't protect an entire city from Torque, but I just can't let this poor guy fry.

There's a screech of tires outside and a long black limo—Gus's limo—pulls up to the curb. Out jumps Torque, and for a moment I actually believe that he knows about this conversation and has come to beat me up for trying to show a little mercy.

"The envelope—" I begin.

"Forget the envelope!" he cuts me off. "Get in the car!" He hustles me out the door and into the limo. "Go!" he growls at the driver.

"What about *my* car?" I protest. "I've got Danny's ride parked around the corner."

"Leave it. We need to get back. Gus took a bad turn. The doctor says he's not going to make it. He wants to see his 'son,' big joke."

The news hits me hard. Sure, I like Gus, but he was always just a means to an end—a guy who might have information we need. That doesn't explain away the feeling I have—like I've swallowed a bowling ball and it's lodged in the pit of my stomach.

I haven't experienced anything like this since the night we escaped Serenity, when I thought Hector was dead. And even that wasn't quite the same. Hector was my best friend at the time, but we weren't related. Okay, Gus isn't my dad and he isn't me. But whatever you call our connection, we're *family*. To a clone, what could be more rare and precious than that?

At the same time, I can't let being sad get in the way of being smart. Laska and I are mixed up with some pretty dangerous people in the Alabaster organization. The only thing that keeps us safe is the fact that the boss thinks I'm his son. Once he's out of the picture, then what? Chances are, Lenny will take over. Lenny's a reasonable guy, and he's always been good to me, but that might be just because Gus wants it. Can I count on that special treatment to continue without Gus around? What about the other guys like Danny and Cyrus and Torque? And how will they react if Torque spills the beans about me lying to them all this time?

My mind spins, turning over all the possibilities and what-ifs. And the conclusion I keep coming to again and again is this: Laska and I have to get away from the Alabaster organization and out of Chicago the instant Gus is gone. I feel guilty about planning and figuring the angles while the man who gave me my DNA lies dying. But nothing is more important than survival.

The problem is Laska is at the soup kitchen, offsetting my life of crime by slinging beans at the dregs of society. It's no good. We need to stick together so we can take off the minute things start to go sour.

I turn to Torque. "First we have to swing by the New Hope Soup Kitchen and pick up Amber."

"No can do," is his bland reply.

"But she'll want to say good-bye to him too."

"My orders are to bring you," he tells me. "Nobody

mentioned anything about your little girlfriend."

I see the freeway ramp coming up on the right. Once we're on that, we're practically home.

Supposedly, I should be able to access all of Gus's famous grit and willpower and backbone. Yet when I search for the toughness to stand up to Torque, it comes not from any gangster, but from Laska herself. What would Amber do? Something wild and reckless—something nobody else would be crazy enough to do.

I throw open the door of the moving limo. "I'm not going without Amber!"

"Shut that door!" he barks.

I undo my seat belt and lean out of the car as mailboxes, streetlights, and garbage cans whiz by. Shocked pedestrians point and stare.

"Go ahead, genius," Torque sneers. "Break every bone in your body. See if I care."

"It's not if *you* care!" I shout, the wind roaring in my ears. "It's if *Gus* cares! He's not going to be too happy if you show up without me!"

The driver is glancing nervously over his shoulder at Torque, unsure of what to do.

"Keep going!" Torque orders. "This wimp hasn't got the guts!"

He's called my bluff—except I'm not bluffing. I'm prepared to go full Laska and jump out of the limo. As I get ready to leap out, all I can think of is how much that pavement is going to hurt when I hit it after exiting a car doing thirty miles an hour.

I squeeze my eyes shut and spring out the door.

An iron grip closes on my collar and hauls me back into the limo. I collapse on the seat, gasping.

"Crazy idiot!" Torque chokes.

All I can manage to wheeze is a raspy, "Amber!"

"Fine! We'll get your girlfriend!"

I'm way too traumatized for any feeling of triumph.

11

AMBER LASKA

I used to be Serenity's biggest fan.

I'm not proud of that, but there it is. I bought into that honesty, harmony, and contentment phony baloney more than anybody else. If any other kid dared to say anything bad about the place, I was the first to jump all over them. Malik called me the Happy Valley cheerleader. You know what? He was right. One of the hardest parts of learning the truth about Project Osiris was this: I lost that feeling of belonging to something wonderful.

Until now.

The New Hope Soup Kitchen isn't an ideal way of life like Serenity pretended to be. It never tries to be more than it is—a safe place that doesn't judge and never threatens, where people in need can get nourishing meals while they struggle to put their lives back together. After all, you can't look for work if you're starving. We don't expect to solve every problem for everybody. But we can at least ensure that hunger isn't making things worse.

I love the people who come to New Hope. Malik puts them down. He calls them bums and hobos and people who talk to telephone poles. This from a kid who hangs out with gangsters and fits in perfectly.

Our customers at the soup kitchen are mostly just like you and me, only they've had some bad luck. Like Dietrich, who never bounced back after he was injured in an industrial accident. Or Selma, whose husband took all their money and disappeared. Or Nathaniel, who used to be an accountant until a small stroke left him unable to do simple arithmetic. There are a few who can't find jobs after being released from prison. Okay, I only started volunteering there to balance out Malik's budding gangster career. But my manager, Ernest, says a lot of the regulars have come to life since then. I can't describe the warm glow that gives me. It means they like me as much as I like them.

The lunch rush is just ending when a new arrival attracts the usual turned heads. But the buzz that greets this newcomer is more charged and nervous than usual. It's a police officer. I'm not thrilled to see him myself. I feel so at home at New Hope that I sometimes forget I'm a fugitive from Project Osiris and the Purple People Eaters. The presence of a uniform jolts my memory in a hurry.

Ernest rushes over to greet the cop. "What can I do for you, officer? I'm the manager."

"Good for you." The policeman is all business. "I'm told this is the place to find Milo Jenkovich. Anybody seen him?"

The clinking of cutlery is suddenly deafening. Heads bow. All attention returns to lunch. I can see Milo at the end of a long table, trying to blend into the crowd. He looks scared.

The cop spots him too. "Long time no see, Milo. I hear you're selling fake Rolexes again."

He starts forward but Ernest steps in his way. "Look, officer. We always cooperate with the police. But this is a safe place, and our clients have to know that they can enjoy a meal without fear. You're welcome to wait for Milo outside. While he's in here, he's under our protection."

The cop is unimpressed. "You're kidding, right?"

I really don't see what he's so annoyed about. Nobody's saying he *can't* talk to Milo; he just can't talk to him *in here*. That's New Hope policy.

Ernest stands his ground. "I'm afraid I'm going to have to ask you to leave."

So the policeman shoves Ernest aside and makes for Milo.

And I see red. The big tray of mashed potatoes is in my hands before I even realize what I'm doing. I heave it over the plastic sneeze guard, raining the entire load down on the advancing cop.

He wheels on me, dripping slop and furious, Milo forgotten. "You're going to regret this, kid!"

He lunges for the counter, and that's all it takes. Everybody in the place—including Milo—jumps up and gets a hand on the cop, holding him back.

I've got a whole speech ready to deliver about respecting the sanctity of New Hope as a safe environment, when Ernest hollers a piece of advice that suddenly makes a lot more sense to someone in my situation: "Run!"

I vault the counter, and blast out the door. As I pound down the block, I'm 100 percent convinced that I did the right thing. I have nothing to apologize for. On the other hand, that cop looked really mad. And for all I know, I'm on the wanted list somewhere. If I get us arrested, Malik will kill me—especially after all the grief I gave *him* about getting us in trouble with the law.

I speed up, running hard, grateful that I've kept in shape. I risk a glance over my shoulder. No sign of pursuit from the cop. But—I frown—a black stretch limo is driving alongside me on the road, keeping pace.

The smoked glass window rolls down, and a familiar voice bawls, *"Amber!"*

Malik.

He throws open the door, grabs my arm, and hauls me inside, whether I want to go or not. In this case, I want to go. Then I see Torque in the car. I still want to be there, but less.

"Where were you running?" Malik demands.

"That's not important," I reply stiffly. "Let's just get out of here."

Torque peers out the back window. "There's a cop outside that sewer you work at. Don't suppose he's looking for you?"

"I kind of attacked him," I admit.

"With what?" Malik demands.

"Mashed potatoes."

Malik stares at me, and I know he's thinking about Mickey Seven.

"It's potatoes, not dynamite." I defend my actions.

"Take us home," Torque orders the driver. He's laughing his head off.

"The doctor says Gus is dying," Malik explains as we accelerate through the traffic. "We're going to see him." He adds meaningfully, "Together."

I nod. We've talked about this. When Gus is gone, we have to be gone too. He's the only reason we're protected in the midst of all these criminals.

"About that," Torque butts in. "Bryan—when you're in there with Gus—"

"I know," Malik says, shamefaced. "I'll tell him the truth."

"No, you won't!" he orders in a commanding voice. "You're the boss's son. When he croaks, you inherit everything!"

"You just want Bryan to inherit Gus's money so you can blackmail him out of it!" I accuse.

Torque casts me an approving smile. "You catch on quick."

"A human being is dying, and you don't even care! He's your boss! Where's your respect?"

The smile disappears. "I respect Gus because he's mean as a cornered pit bull, and he'd whack me as soon as look at me if he felt like it. But pretty soon he's going to be out of the picture. And what we've got here"—he indicates Malik—"is a career advancement plan."

The limo wheels onto Ramsey Road, and pulls up in front of the palatial Alabaster home. The long circular drive is parked solid with expensive sports cars. The troops are all here to see the general into the next world.

Suddenly, the shiny gold decor seems like nothing more than the out-of-date trappings of a dying empire. Gus's suite is packed with crooks, standing around with solemn faces. At the place of honor, next to the bed, is Lenny.

Gus looks terrible. His face is paler than the white of his sheets, and the simple effort of keeping his eyes open seems to take all the strength he has. The tubes and monitors have all been removed. Nobody needs to be told the state of this man's health. Even the doctor is hovering in the background, a spectator. There's nothing more that he can do.

Spying Malik, Lenny waves us over. Big, tough Malik looks about five years old as he shuffles his way to the bed.

Gus's ravaged face lights up when he spies Malik. He whispers something to Lenny, and Lenny clears the room and follows everyone else outside. I try to exit with the others, but Malik grabs my arm and keeps me with him.

No way he's facing this alone. The last thing we see before Lenny closes the door is a warning look from Torque.

When Gus finally speaks, his voice is like crackling paper. "I didn't get to be a father for very long."

Even I feel bad for him, and I know for a fact that he's one of the worst criminal masterminds ever. I can tell Malik is working hard not to cry.

"But I'm glad we got . . . these last few days, Bryan." The gangster has to pause and catch his breath just to manage a full sentence. "It makes this dying business a little easier . . . knowing I have a son."

I give Malik a quick kidney punch. "Tell him!" I whisper.

Gus may be on the way out, but there's nothing wrong with the old guy's ears. "Tell me what?"

Malik wants to strangle me, but he knows I'm right. "Gus—" A tremor in his voice. "There's no easy way to say this. I'm not your kid." Involuntarily, he takes a half step back. Maybe he expects Gus to call in his boys to spray the room with machine-gun fire.

The old man looks sad, but manages a chuckle between gasps. "Got to hand it to you, Bryan . . . You really had me going. Funny—I could have sworn you . . . looked just like me. Goes to show how much I . . . wanted it to be true."

"It *is* true!" Malik blurts. "I mean—not the way you think it is." He swallows hard. "Have you ever heard of Project Osiris?"

Gus frowns, thinking hard. All at once, his eyes, which were practically closed, widen into a shocked stare. "Osiris? They did it? That's *you*?"

We both nod.

"So you're not my son. You're . . . *me*?"

"Physically, anyway," Malik confirms. "You as a kid."

The mob boss digests all this.

"Sorry," Malik murmurs. "I shouldn't have lied to you."

"Are you kidding?" Despite his feebleness, Gus breaks into a grin. "This is even better! It's like I'm . . . still alive, out of jail. And the cops will never know!"

I speak up. "Can you tell us what you remember about Osiris at the very beginning? They approached you in prison, right?"

"I thought it was all . . . hot air. Cloning? What is this, *Star Wars*? . . . But she offered to get me transferred from North Carolina to Joliet—my own backyard. And the procedure was nothing—like getting a flu shot. She said it might not . . . even work." He slumps back onto the pillow, exhausted from this speech. "So I forgot the whole thing."

Malik's eyes meet mine.

"She?" he asks. "Didn't you meet a guy named Felix Hammerstrom?"

Gus tries to shake his head, although he only moves a fraction of an inch. "This was a lady—a real rich broad. Said she started some big computer company."

"You mean *Tamara Dunleavy*?" I breathe.

"That's the one. Fancy type. Full of herself."

It's a major shock. When we tracked down Tamara Dunleavy in Jackson Hole, she swore she'd never heard of Project Osiris. We were pretty sure she was lying. Now we have proof.

Gus is still smiling. "I envy you, Bryan. You've got . . . my whole life ahead of you." He looks pleased with that clever remark.

Malik shoots me a sideways glance, and I can read what he's thinking. He may have come to Chicago admiring the gangster lifestyle. But now that he's had a taste of it, he knows it's not for him. Malik and I weren't friends in Serenity, and we've been fighting nonstop since we broke out. But I've never been as proud of him as I am at this moment.

"I'll try to use it well," Malik promises in a strangled voice.

Gus closes his eyes for a moment. Then, in an incredible

show of determination, he lifts his wasted body halfway to a sitting position, and peers into Malik's eyes, a match for his own. "Listen to me!" he croaks urgently.

"What, Gus?"

Malik leans over and the old man whispers something into his ear. Then Gus falls back to the bed and lies unmoving.

Malik is still poised over him, waiting for more.

"I think he's gone, Malik," I say quietly.

He's shell-shocked.

"I'm sorry."

His eyes never leave Gus's inert form.

"We better tell Lenny," I add. "He's in charge of everything now."

His face pale, Malik crosses the room to open the bedroom door. Standing there with Lenny and the rest of the crew are two policemen.

Malik's face is suffused with outrage. "You cops are something else! Can't a guy be dead for ten seconds before you vultures pounce on him?"

But I've already recognized one of the cops by the mashed potato smears on his uniform. He must have seen me get into the limo and checked to see who the license plate was registered to.

"They're not here for Gus," Lenny explains. "They're here for the girl."

I'll bet even Mickey Seven never managed this one. Surrounded by the most notorious crime organization in the country, and the only person under arrest is me.

12

ELI FRIEDEN

The second time I meet Blake Upton is in our little bun-galow on the Atomic Studios lot. Tori brings him in and plunks him down on the couch. Even though Tori said she would do it, I have to admit I'm pretty blown away when it really happens. Apparently, she can get her hands on people the way Yvonne-Marie Delacroix got her hands on people's money.

Blake looks uncomfortable, but he's here, and that's all that matters.

I try to put him at ease. "Sorry for pretending to be you. We had to get your attention."

"Well, you got it," he growls. "My manager's fielding complaints that my autographs are fake because they don't match yours, which are all over Twitter. Thanks a lot."

"Sorry," I repeat. I guess Twitter is even more important in the outside world than I thought.

"The point is," Tori interrupts briskly, "that the two of you look too much alike for it to be a coincidence. Like it or not, you're both related to Bartholomew Glen."

He doesn't say yes, but he doesn't say no either. "Not according to my parents. They also told me there's nobody in the family who could be my twin."

"All those people on Twitter don't think so," Tori reminds him.

His shoulders slump. "What do you want from me?"

"Bartholomew Glen is at Noranda State Penitentiary, about seventy miles from here," I reply. "We have to go see him."

His eyes widen. "You want to go to a *jail* to visit a *serial killer*? Why?"

"He must be the missing link between us."

"If we're so identical, what do you need me for?" Blake challenges. "Go yourself and tell him to multiply by two."

"You have to be there," I insist, sticking to the story of myself as an orphan. "I've got no past, but you do. If we can get this guy to talk about himself, you might recognize an old family memory or a distant relative or something."

He has another concern. "Will they let us in to see this

guy? Don't we have to be on some kind of visitors list?"

"You're already on it," Tori informs him.

He gawks at us in disbelief.

"I've got kind of a knack with computers," I supply.

"You *hacked* in?" His famous face—our face—screws up like he's about to bawl. "To a *jail*?"

Actually, it isn't even a new experience for me. I hacked into the Kefauver Federal Detention Facility when we busted C. J. Rackoff out. But I keep my mouth shut.

"And if I say no?" he persists.

Tori's voice stays friendly, but she's firm. "How could you not want to know?"

He's defiant. "I do want to know," he admits. "I just wish there was a better way than showing up at the state pen and asking to see the biggest psycho there."

"It creeps me out too," I confess. "But it's the only way."

At least Blake is probably just a relative. I'm the psycho's second coming.

Twenty minutes later, Blake and I are on the freeway, heading north in the chauffeured car the studio provides for him. That's definitely safer than taking the sedan we stole in Amarillo—especially since we'll be rolling up to a place that's surrounded by security cameras. And anyway, I'm relieved that I don't have to explain why I'm driving when Blake doesn't even have a license, and I'm younger than him.

It's just the two of us in the backseat. We left Tori in the bungalow. Noranda is a maximum-security prison, and Bartholomew Glen is surely its most maximum-security inmate. In Texas, it was pretty easy to visit C. J. Rackoff, who Hector was cloned from. But that was medium security, and Rackoff never killed anybody; he just bamboozled them. He sure bamboozled us. An audience with a serial killer is probably harder to get. It'll be tough enough for two of us to get in. Three might have put us over the top— especially if the third was a twelve-year-old girl.

It's an uncomfortable trip, even though the car is pretty cushy. Blake and I have nothing to say to each other, and for sure nothing we want the driver to hear. As it is, the man's not too thrilled about driving a couple of kids to a notorious jail.

After a very long silence, Blake bursts out with, "What are you going to say to him?"

For once, I'm able to be honest. "I'm kind of hoping he'll recognize us and solve the mystery right away."

He nods. "Even if that doesn't happen, he's bound to notice how much we look alike. So maybe that'll be a starting point for the conversation."

It's the first sign ever that Blake is actually on board with what we're about to do. He still hates me—or at least hates what I represent. I was probably the first sour note in his perfect life. He's famous, everybody loves him, he's starting to get rich—I think TV stars make a lot of money. If Tori and I hadn't forced him into this, he would have loved to pretend I didn't exist. Now, though, it's like he's finally accepted that there's something going on that we have to get to the bottom of. We're not allies, exactly, and we'll never be friends. But at least we have a common goal. It makes me feel slightly less alone.

Noranda State Penitentiary is like an immense gray cube that dropped from the sky and buried itself three-quarters of the way into the California landscape. There are no fences or towers or prison yards, just vast windowless concrete walls. I remember thinking that C. J. Rackoff's prison in Texas had to be the most awful place on earth. I stand corrected. The unfortunate inmates here never see the light of day. Not that someone like Bartholomew Glen, who killed nine people, deserves to be treated as anything but the animal he is.

"Wow," Blake breathes. "Remind me never to break the law."

"This isn't for your average cheap crook," our driver tosses over his shoulder. "This is for people who've forfeited the right to be human."

And I'm an exact copy of the worst of them.

Even though we're on the list, we're questioned, searched, questioned again, and led through a metal detector. We tell our cover story at least two dozen times: No, we're not twins, but we are brothers. Blake is fourteen months older. Bartholomew Glen is our mother's brother. This is the first time she's given us the okay to visit our infamous uncle. We hand over the phone number of our bungalow at Atomic Studios so they can call "Mom" for confirmation. They actually call, and I bite my lip for a couple of anxious minutes while the supervisor talks to Tori.

I shouldn't have worried. No one lies like the clone of Yvonne-Marie Delacroix.

The supervisor hangs up. "All right, you two. Follow me."

He leads us into a meeting room that looks totally normal at first. Then I realize that the space is cut in half by a thick sheet of bulletproof glass. There are holes, which look like bubbles hanging in the air, so that sound can pass through. A sharp snap behind us indicates that we've been locked in.

Blake looks uncomfortable. "Amos will kill me if he ever finds out about this."

I bite back my own dread. What do I have to fear from Bartholomew Glen? I'm exactly him, only younger and stronger.

We're alone there for a long time, too scared to speak, even to each other. It's at least twenty minutes—and feels like twenty months—when the door opens on the other side of the glass, and the Crossword Killer is just a few yards away from us.

Killer. The word reverberates inside my mind. The Osiris subjects are all cloned from criminals, but even among that group, Bartholomew Glen stands out. Sure, there were many deaths from Mickey Seven's bombings; Yvonne-Marie Delacroix's daring robberies claimed casualties; Gus Alabaster ordered hits on his gangland enemies; and people were certainly ruined in C. J. Rackoff's frauds and swindles, even if nobody actually died. This man is different. The lives he took were not in pursuit of any goal, regardless of how horrible or lawless. He killed for the sake of killing. Nothing could be worse than that.

I don't know what I expect him to look like, but this isn't it. I remember an internet photograph of a wild-eyed maniac with a shaved head. Bartholomew Glen is bald, but that's where the resemblance ends. First off, he's a lot smaller than I expected, compact, yet physically fit. His eyes are interested, alive, and reveal a keen intelligence. His expression is open, almost friendly.

He looks back and forth between Blake and me. "Which one of you is Jesse Jordan?"

Blake's jaw drops. "You watch *Jupiter High*?"

"I watch everything. I have a lot of spare time." There's something about Glen's tone that I can't quite put my finger on. Then it hits me. It's not tone; it's pronunciation. Every syllable is enunciated to perfection. The eyes stop on Blake. "I believe it's you. And this one"—indicating me—"a brother?"

I've come so far and been through so much to see this man. But now that I'm in front of him, I'm struck dumb. It's weird—I've only been in Glen's presence a few seconds, but I know that *he* would never be struck dumb. His sharp mind would always have something to say. Why am I so different? I'm supposed to be the same person.

Maybe it's the fact that I'm finally confronted with my genetic donor—the person whose DNA created me. Much closer than any parent, he's actually me—an older version, anyway. I realize that, from the moment I first learned I was a clone, everything in my life was building up to this meeting.

Blake shoots me a sharp glance. Since this whole thing was my idea, he wasn't expecting me to clam up. "I'm an only child," he supplies. "We came to you because we were wondering—well, maybe you could explain how come we look so much alike."

Bartholomew Glen is one of those people who's always thinking, calculating almost. It's right there on his face— he's sizing up every situation, figuring the angles for his best advantage. But like a computer that's been given an instruction that makes no sense, he's confused by Blake's words. "*I* can explain why *you* look alike?"

"You—you know"—Blake's stammering a little— "because you guys are related."

The Crossword Killer's penetrating gaze shifts to me, and he folds his arms in front of him. "Do tell."

I find my voice at last. "What do you remember about an experiment called Project Osiris?"

His arched eyebrows shoot up. "Osiris! I recall it well." He regards us, head tilted. "You two—a clone, perhaps? And a second-generation clone?"

Blake's expression is pure shock.

He gets even redder when I say, "I'm the clone. He's real."

Blake is sputtering now. "You're a *clone*? Of *me*?"

I shake my head sadly. "No. Of him."

A slow smile of understanding spreads over Glen's pale face. "So that's why you boys came to see me. I have an answer for you. Would you like to hear it?"

It's the last thing on earth I want to hear. But if it sheds any light on who or what I am, I need to know. "Tell me."

"I was the first candidate approached by this lunatic scheme, their top pick, if you will. I refused, of course. There can only ever be one of me. I am unique."

I gawk at him. "I'm not your clone?"

"You're welcome," he tells me sarcastically. "No one can be cloned from DNA that was never harvested. That ridiculous woman couldn't seem to accept that all her billions could not purchase a single cell from my body."

Hope surges inside me. I'm not an exact replica of this horror show? Suddenly, I've never wanted anything to be true quite so much. "Billions," I manage, heart pounding. "You're talking about Tamara Dunleavy."

"Tamara Dunleavy?" Blake blurts. "She's my dad's aunt!"

I have a giddy vision of the one time we met the tech

billionaire—the time she told us she'd never heard of any Project Osiris. She stared at me like she couldn't take her eyes off me. We all noticed it. Now I understand why. I'm a dead ringer for her grandnephew.

Glen laughs out loud. "Well? Are you there yet? Have you figured it out?"

I'm so emotionally drained that I haven't gotten past the fact that I'm not the Crossword Killer, version 2.0.

Blake's even more confused than I am. "How do you guys both know my aunt Tammy?"

Glen seems highly amused. "Quite a puzzle, isn't it? I suppose I'll have to solve it for you. When Ms. Dunleavy was unable to acquire my DNA, she must have used her own. That explains the family resemblance between the two of you. You're not my clone; you're hers."

"But—but—that's impossible!" I stammer. "I can't be cloned from her! I'm a *guy*!"

Glen smiles tolerantly. "A lab capable of human cloning might be capable of taking the next logical step—converting female to male."

"You can do that?" I ask, aghast.

"We're already talking about rogue science here," he explains pleasantly. "Highly illegal, but equally brilliant. An XX chromosome is what makes a person female. If that were to be altered to XY, the clone of a woman would be born male. You are identical to Tamara Dunleavy in every way except your gender. I hope this means you can get your hands on some of those billions."

The floor tilts under my feet, and it's all I can do to remain upright. It's crazy, but in a way, it makes perfect sense. I have nothing in common with a guy who kills people and designs crossword puzzles about it. But a computer innovator—that's me in every way.

Blake is staring at me. "This is too weird! You're not my aunt! You can't be! There are no clones! Just that sheep, right? The one in England?"

He looks so baffled that I can't help feeling sorry for him. This has to be a whole lot worse than just seeing yourself giving autographs on Twitter when you know it isn't you.

"I understand why you're an actor," the Crossword Killer comments mildly to Blake. "You have no imagination so you require a writer to put words in your mouth."

"Stop it!" I snap. "Can't you see the guy's upset?" I pound on the door behind us. "Guard! Guard! We're done here!"

"So soon?" Glen queries. "This is just starting to get interesting. For example, since there's you, I deduce that there are others like you. And not all of them were spliced off a tech billionaire. I'm guessing there were other candidates to donate DNA, and at least some lacked the willpower to say no. Who can imagine what Little League of supervillains might be loose upon the world?"

"You're wrong," I shoot back. "The experiment was evil, but we're not villains."

The door opens and the guard hustles us out. The last words I hear from the Crossword Killer chill me to the bone.

"So far . . ."

We're still kids. It's early yet. Who knows better than this man how it feels to be a criminal mastermind? He wasn't murdering yet when he was our age. Plenty of time to fulfill the horrible promise of our DNA.

Except me. My DNA is pure tech wizard. The only criminal part is the part that collaborated with Felix Hammerstrom to dream up Project Osiris. Which might be just as twisted, when you think about it.

We pass through the various layers of security and eventually make our way out to the car.

"So," asks the chauffeur, "how did it go?"

"Take us back to the studio," is the only answer he gets from Blake.

We get in the limo only to get out again so the gate sentries can search it. And it's not just the trunk. They pull off the seats and examine the undercarriage with mirrors. I'm not even impatient. If this is what it takes to keep Bartholomew Glen where he belongs, I'm all for it.

The shock is fading, and in its place, pure relief is pouring in. Twenty minutes ago, I believed I was an exact replica of the worst person on earth, and now I know I'm *not*.

I'm not, I'm not, I'm not!

At last, we're on the freeway, heading south toward LA. Blake looks so agitated that I figure I owe him an explanation, especially since I lured him here without ever once mentioning the word *clone*.

I close the partition so the driver can't overhear us, and face him across the backseat. "We're not monsters, you know. We're a hundred percent human, even though we didn't start out the same way as everybody else. I'm sorry to drag you into it. But something really awful was done to us, and we have to try to get to the bottom of it."

It does nothing to settle him down. "So are we, like, cousins or something?"

"Actually, I think I'm your great aunt," I tell him ruefully. "But since I'm a guy, maybe it counts as uncle. I'm still fuzzy on that one. I just found out about it myself."

I can tell he's working hard to keep his anger under control. "You asked me to go with you, and I went. Now I want you out of my life. Take your girlfriend and get away from my studio. And if I ever hear about you posing as me again, I'm calling the cops."

I suppose I should be insulted, but I can't really blame him. I yanked him out of his comfortable life and dropped him into the insanity that's Project Osiris. And it's all so weird that he can't even tell anybody about me—not without looking crazy himself.

"That's good for me too," I assure him. "We'll be out of your hair as soon as I pick up Tori. You'll never see me again." I'm guessing we won't ever end up sitting across from each other at Tamara Dunleavy's Thanksgiving dinner table.

Tamara Dunleavy! I'm still having trouble wrapping my mind around it. Sure, it's better than being cloned from a bank robber or a terrorist or mob boss—and a huge boost from Bartholomew Glen. But the Osiris experiment was all about cloning master criminals. Why would she use her own DNA?

Soon, the freeways widen, and I can tell we're in the suburbs of Los Angeles. Then the car is tooling along the palm tree–lined boulevard that leads to Atomic Studios.

"I'll make sure you get in the gate and back to your girl," Blake says to me. "After that, I want you gone."

"Promise." The least I can do is leave him alone.

Soon, we're on studio property, pulling to the curb at Bungalow 149.

I start up the walkway. He calls after me, "I'm glad you didn't turn out to be that Glen guy."

"Me too," I reply with a little smile.

The window whispers shut and the car moves off.

I give the secret knock and get no answer. When I try the knob, the door swings wide. I frown. It's not like Tori to be so careless. But I'm practically bursting to tell her. It's not every day a guy learns he's not cloned from a serial killer.

She's sitting behind the desk, and the look on her face tells me, without a word, that something is very wrong. I take a step toward her, and she shakes her head no. That's when I notice the duct tape wrapped around her arms, imprisoning her in the chair.

Two tall men in dark suits burst out of the other room.

"Run, Eli!" Tori cries.

Yet running never even occurs to me. In my mind, being separated is worse than being captured. Whatever happens to her has to happen to me too.

Knowing it's hopeless, I prepare to fight for both of us. I turn on our attackers, assuming they must be Purple People Eaters. But instead, I recognize them as the two who tried to kidnap Tori from that parking lot in Amarillo.

I pick up the nearest object—a floor lamp—and swing it at them. It turns out to be a mistake. The bigger one grabs it and hauls me in like a fish on a line. Desperately, I bury my elbow in his stomach. The guy doesn't even flinch. Powerful arms imprison me, and soon I find myself duct-taped too, my arms locked behind my back.

I say the first thing that comes to mind. "If anything happens to us, you'll never see your car again!"

They laugh like I've just told the funniest joke in the world. The next piece of duct tape goes over my mouth. Tori is silenced too, so at least she can't accuse me of putting up a lousy fight.

They toss us in the back of a closed panel truck marked *FLARE STUNT SERVICES AND PYROTECHNICS* and throw a tarp over us. I'm on the verge of losing it. If we're going back to Project Osiris, then everything we've been through was for nothing. And with Malik and Amber already captured—or worse—we represent the last hope that the Osiris clones will get any kind of justice. All that's gone now.

The drive is endless—or maybe it just feels that way because of our fear of what lies at the end of it. Our brief time away from Serenity was far from fun, but it was freedom, and that means everything. Conversation is impossible, but I can read the desolation in Tori's eyes. Is this where our quest comes to an end? Taped up in the back of a stunt truck?

At long last, we seem to go down a ramp, and after a few quick turns, come to a stop. Our captors get out of the cab. A moment later, the payload doors swing wide and the tarp is pulled off us.

I sit up, expecting to see Felix Hammerstrom and some of the other Osiris parents.

Our two captors haul us out of the truck and stand us up on the concrete of a dimly lit parking garage.

Out of the gloom, a figure comes walking toward us—a tall older woman dressed in an elegant business suit and immaculate white sneakers.

Tamara Dunleavy.

13

MALIK BRUDER

Laska!

Why did I have to get paired up with her? I'm amazed that prison in Florida where they've got Mickey Seven hasn't melted down into the earth's core just because there's someone like Laska locked up there.

You're going to get us arrested! She must have told me that fifty times. Sure enough, here we are, arrested. And who got us that way? Laska.

I should have hung her out to dry when that cop showed up at Gus's place. He wasn't there to bust *me*. I didn't dump mashed potatoes on anybody. It would have been the easi-est thing in the world to blend in with Lenny and the guys while Laska got marched away in handcuffs. *What, her? Never seen her before in my life.*

That's my problem—I'm too nice. And that means Gus was probably nice too. Everybody says he was this ruthless, psycho mob boss, but deep down, I think he was just like me. Too bad I didn't get to know him better.

His last words keep haunting me. Not because they were so scary or anything like that, but because they made zero sense. Maybe that's because he was already starting to die, so his mind was shutting down. I was hoping his message would turn out to be that he regretted his life of crime, because, in his heart, he was a pretty good guy. That might have helped me feel a little better about the whole death part. Or not. Who knows? Watching the person you're cloned from croak right in front of you is a weird experience. And it's not like there's somebody I can talk to about it, since I'm the only one it's ever happened to.

Whatever. There's no point in rehashing all that. When that cop put the cuffs on Laska, I went with them, stupid me. I was so shaken up by Gus biting the big one that it never occurred to me that the real problem wasn't who threw mashed potatoes on who. It was the fact that we're two kids with no ID, no parents, no home. They aren't going to cut us loose until they have an adult to take charge of us. That's never going to happen. Or maybe it is, which would be even worse. If Chicago PD has us all over the internet as these poor lost kids, eventually Project Osiris is going to send somebody to reel us in.

So here I am, sitting next to Laska in the interrogation room. I can't begin to guess how long we've been here. Long enough to be fed stale sandwiches three times, and watch the shift change at least twice. At first, they questioned us separately, so they could check to see if our stories matched. We didn't give them any stories. Even Laska has the brains to keep her big mouth shut for a change.

The craziest part is this: Amber doesn't regret anything. In her mind, that cop was violating the rules of the soup kitchen, and she had the obligation to stop him any way she could. In this case, with mashed potatoes.

"It's not about the potatoes!" I hiss at her, pretty sure the room is bugged. "Don't you understand? We're kids! They're not going to let us go till they can turn us over to a parent or guardian. Best-case scenario, we both wind up in orphanages. Worst case, it's the Purples."

She's been defiant all day, but the hours and hours of interrogation have finally worn her down. Her face falls. "I'm sorry, Malik. This is completely my fault."

And then two big tears roll down her cheeks. Laska— who wouldn't cry if you poured molten lava over her head. So instead of letting her have it, I tell her, "It's my fault too.

Maybe we can still get out of this." Like I said, too nice.

The snap of the lock makes both of us jump. The door opens and in walks the mashed potatoes cop. He must have started a new shift, since he has a fresh uniform on. He's accompanied by a partner, a younger woman who looks huge in her bulletproof vest.

"How long do we have to stay here?" I ask.

Wordlessly, they handcuff us both behind our backs and march us out of the interrogation room. I see a third officer feeding our file into a large paper shredder.

"Why are you destroying our file?" Amber demands. "What are you going to do to us?"

"It was only mashed potatoes!" I add.

We get no answer. They guide us through the police station, out to the parking lot, and stuff us into a squad car. Danny and Torque talked about this once—how "going for a ride" doesn't mean sightseeing. The guy in the backseat is only traveling one way. It's something that happens in Gus's world, but I never would have believed the police do it too.

"Listen," I whisper as we pull out into traffic. "The minute they let us out of the car, we run."

"No talking," Mashed Potatoes calls over his shoulder.

We drive for maybe ten or fifteen minutes—it's hard to estimate time when you're scared out of your mind.

It's a clear day. The sun is high in the sky. I'm guessing it's early afternoon. Danny and Torque never gave details about where these "rides" end up, but I'm picturing woods, where no one can see what you're doing. This is definitely not that—we're still in the city. The tall buildings of downtown are no more than a couple of miles away.

We drive in through a very high gate to a small private airport. The car moves straight up to a gleaming Gulfstream jet and stops. Okay, so we're not about to be murdered, but this could be even worse. A private plane, police cooperation—it has Project Osiris written all over it.

The two cops haul us out of the backseat and remove our handcuffs. I look at Laska and mumble a single word. "Now."

We take off like a couple of gazelles, sprinting flat out. She's faster than me, so I get tackled first. I leave a lot of my chin and at least one elbow on the tarmac. Lying there bleeding, Mashed Potatoes' knee in the small of my back, I watch as Laska almost makes it to the gate.

She must see what happened to me, because she hesitates.

I shout, "Keep running!" but it's too late. The lady cop brings her down.

Amber struggles against her all the way back. Mickey

Seven to the end. I'm almost proud of her, which is stupid, considering she's to blame for the trouble we're in. We're frog-marched to the jet, up the fold-down stairs, and forced into the cabin.

Amber freezes and I smack into her from behind. I can sense her whole body recoiling in shock.

"Tori!" she breathes.

It's Tori, who we haven't seen since we took off down that river in Texas. Eli's there too. He's actually wearing a smile, instead of his usual computer-screen coma.

"We thought you were dead!" the four of us blurt, practically in unison.

The girls leap into each other's arms. I clap Frieden on the shoulder. But in the middle of this happy reunion, it hits me. Eli and Tori were either dead or captured. Since they're not dead, that leaves caught. And if they're caught, so are we.

I motion toward the closed cockpit door and murmur, "Purples?"

"Not exactly—" Eli begins.

And then the last thing I expect happens. A hatch from a private cabin opens and out steps Tamara Dunleavy. Suddenly, everything makes sense—this must be *her* plane! I should have known. The stuff she told us about splitting from Osiris—pure baloney. She founded it and she's been pulling the strings from day one! And Hammerstrom and the others work for her!

"Liar!" I accuse. "You said you never heard of Osiris! You *are* Osiris!"

Eli wraps his arms around me and plants his shoulder in the center of my chest to keep me from rushing at the founder of VistaNet. "Malik—it's okay! She's on our side!"

"Why would you believe anything she tells you?" I roar. "All those years we sat in Happy Valley, taking Contentment class and being studied by people who pretended to be our parents—*she* was behind that! Every time we pledged allegiance with unity and gladness for all! And you don't think she deserves to be tossed out of this jet at thirty thousand feet?"

"Malik!" Tori exclaims. "Calm down!"

"Calm? I'm Gus Alabaster, remember? Nobody knows that better than her!" I turn furious eyes on the billionaire. "*You're* the one who hit Gus up for my DNA! He told me himself, so don't try to deny it!"

I'm just getting started, but when I stop to catch my breath for more yelling, Tamara Dunleavy surprises me again by saying quietly, "You're absolutely right."

"Huh?"

"I lied when I said I'd never heard of Project Osiris," she confesses. "And it's true that I cofounded the whole thing—Felix and I. But I dropped out when I realized what an unethical experiment it was. And I assumed that it had been canceled when I withdrew the financial backing. When you kids found me in Jackson Hole, I was so shocked that my first impulse was to deny everything."

"They got the money anyway," Amber supplies. "C. J. Rackoff had it in secret bank accounts."

"Rackoff," Ms. Dunleavy repeats. "One of our original DNA donor candidates. Not a murderer, but a merciless swindler. It's a good thing he'll never see the light of day again."

"Actually," Frieden admits, "we broke him out of jail. He promised to help us tell our story to the world. He tricked us—him and Hector, his clone."

Ms. Dunleavy takes this in. "So now there are two of him out there."

Maybe, as the gangster guy, I'm a thug at heart, not a thinker. But there's one question that's been bugging me ever since I found out who and what I am. "Okay, so you dropped out of Osiris when you realized it was bad. But before that, you must have thought it was good. What made you want to do it in the first place?"

She's silent for a long moment. "I had a younger brother—Jonas," she replies finally. "A good boy; a sweet boy. But with a wild side. He got mixed up with the wrong crowd and wound up in prison for a petty theft." Her face tightens. "He was killed by another inmate. The news shattered my family. Jonas wasn't evil—just foolish. He needed *guidance*. That's what the justice system should have provided. I thought Project Osiris could change things—prove to the corrections system that their focus should be on rehabilitation, not punishment."

"How does cloning crooks do that?" asks Laska.

"By proving that no one has evil in their DNA. If exact genetic copies of criminals could be raised to be good people, then anyone could be reformed with positive nurturing instead of long prison sentences." She sighs emotionally. "It was a brilliant hypothesis. No one could ever say that Felix Hammerstrom isn't a gifted scientist."

"Unless you're one of the freaks they cooked up to make a point," I put in bitterly. We Alabasters aren't the forgiving type.

Ms. Dunleavy nods sadly. "I came to realize that. I should have seen it sooner, but I was obsessed with getting justice for my brother after the fact. And anyway, I was positive the whole thing had died out." She turns to Eli. "And when you appeared—a virtual twin of my grandnephew, claiming to be an Osiris clone—I knew that Felix had done the unthinkable and cloned *me*."

That gets my attention. "Cloned *you*? What's up with that? Frieden's cloned from that Glen guy—the Crossword Killer."

She shakes her head. "The Osiris committee considered Glen. He refused to participate. No, Eli is cloned from me. There's no other explanation. His gender must have been altered in the process—probably Felix's ploy to keep me from learning the truth if I ever stumbled on the project."

"But I thought the whole idea was to clone criminals," I remind her. "You're not a criminal; you started a computer company."

Ms. Dunleavy looks away uncomfortably. "That's where you're wrong. Before I built VistaNet, I was a plain hacker—one of the worst, because I was one of the best."

"I've got kind of a knack for that too," Frieden volunteers, embarrassed.

"I thought I was smarter than everybody else," she goes on. "I wanted to knock governments and big corporations down a peg. I designed viruses to black out power grids, air traffic control systems, vital communications. Plenty of people got hurt, maybe even died, because of the chaos I created. I've been trying to make up for it with charity work ever since."

Ha! What do you know? Turns out the great and celebrated Tamara Dunleavy has trashy DNA just like the rest of us. Suddenly, I don't feel so bad about jacking her Bentley and taking it for a joyride all over the west.

Amber speaks up. "So what happens now?"

"I'm not going to pretend that I can undo what's been done to you," she tells us honestly. "But I can help you."

That rubs me the wrong way. "Listen, we blew the lid off Project Osiris and busted out of Happy Valley all by ourselves. And we've been making the Purples eat our dust ever since. We don't want your help, lady. You've helped enough already."

"Malik," Tori says gently, "she *rescued* us."

"If it wasn't for her, we wouldn't have needed rescuing," I shoot back.

"Maybe not," Ms. Dunleavy admits. "But you need what I can offer you now."

"Fine," Laska agrees. "Come with us to the police to back up our story about Project Osiris. Hammerstrom and our so-called 'parents'—they have to pay for this!"

The billionaire shakes her head sadly. "Felix knows

about my hacker past. If I turn the authorities on him, he'll turn them right back on me."

I bristle. "No offense, but that's *your* problem. None of us hacked into anything—except maybe Frieden a couple of times. And that was only to save our butts."

She sighs. "I'm afraid my problem *is* your problem. Even if everyone associated with Osiris went to prison, your biggest obstacle would remain—the fact that you're kids. You're too young to get a job or rent an apartment or do any of the things that make up a normal life. That's what I can do for you. Come and live with me, and I'll take care of you until you're old enough to take care of yourselves. But if I'm arrested too, that possibility disappears."

Man, that burns me up. She got us into this mess, and now we have to protect her secret because she's the only one who can get us out of it. Still, there's no arguing against her logic. Say what you want about the gangster life-style—nobody can claim those guys aren't realistic when somebody else holds all the power. Back in Chicago, when Torque had something on me, I had to lick his boots. Now we're all going to have to do that with Tamara Dunleavy's ultra-white sneakers.

I cast a glance over at Laska. If anybody is going to hate the idea of moving in with the cofounder of Project Osiris, it'll be her. She doesn't look happy, but she isn't going ape either, ranting and raging about justice.

"There are seven more of us, you know," Eli points out. "We don't know where they are, but they're probably still with Hammerstrom and Project Osiris."

"I'll make some inquiries," Ms. Dunleavy promises. "I'll hire private investigators if I have to. We might be able to find them."

"If you find Hector, leave him to rot," I growl.

Ms. Dunleavy spreads her arms in a questioning gesture. "So, do I tell the pilot to lay in a flight plan for Jackson Hole?"

We look at each other. It's not perfect, not even close. When you're a victim of something like Project Osiris, hiding out on some billionaire's estate doesn't feel like the happy ending you're yearning for. But it's tough to ignore the advantages—a roof over our heads; three square meals a day; no looking over our shoulders for the cops, or worse, the Purple People Eaters.

Tori makes the final decision for all of us. She takes a seat and fastens her belt. "It's a deal."

14

ELI FRIEDEN

The Bentley is back. We took it all the way to New Mexico, but Ms. Dunleavy got it returned somehow. Billionaires make stuff happen.

"It's good to see you, buddy," Malik tells the car every time he lays eyes on it. He also pats the hood. I think that Bentley might be his favorite thing in the whole world. He definitely likes it more than he likes us.

Vachon, the chauffeur, isn't a big fan of ours, which is pretty understandable. He was in charge of the Bentley when we stole it. We left him unconscious in a park. He has no choice but to accept us, though. Ms. Dunleavy told all her staff that we're underprivileged orphans she's taking in as part of her charity work. Vachon knows there has to be more to it than that, but not the truth about who we really are. Nobody has that information except Ms. Dunleavy herself. And, out there somewhere, Project Osiris.

The one word that best describes how our lives have changed is *safe*. Here on Ms. Dunleavy's sprawling property in the mountains near Jackson Hole, we don't have to agonize about the Purple People Eaters coming to scoop us up. We don't have to worry that some police officer is going to question why a bunch of kids are living on their own. We don't have to think about food in our stomachs or shelter. I never realized how much that fear had become part of me ever since we escaped Serenity. I still wake up with that gnawing in my gut, and I have to assure myself I've got nothing to be afraid of. It's a pretty wonderful thing.

In Serenity, the houses we grew up in were super-nice, but that doesn't begin to compare with how a billionaire gets to live. Even Malik and Amber, who stayed in Gus Alabaster's mansion, say it was nothing like this. The Dunleavy home is ultra-modern, with gigantic windows that bring the spectacular scenery indoors. It has its own movie theater, an indoor pool, tennis and basketball courts, and a fully equipped gym. There are two kitchens—one just for snacks, the other for the professional cook and his staff. The place is so big that it's a workout just to walk from one side to the other.

Speaking of workouts, Amber is in heaven. She's making up for all the exercise she didn't get during our life on the run. Every time I see her, she's either soaking wet from the pool, sweat-covered from the gym, or heading out for a jog through the miles of alpine trails on the property. One of the security guys has to go with her when she leaves the house—a rule that applies to the four of us. Project Osiris is still out there, and Ms. Dunleavy isn't taking any chances.

Malik loves it here too, but he's the opposite of Amber. As active as she is, he seems determined to move as little as possible.

"I moved already," he explains righteously, as if he was the only one who escaped Serenity and the Purples. "In the last few weeks, I moved enough for five lifetimes. And now I'm exercising my constitutional right to sit on my butt."

The mountainous terrain of Jackson Hole makes this the perfect place for Tori to get back to her artwork.

Every afternoon she returns to the house with a new canvas to show us. "This is the most beautiful scenery I've ever seen. But what I'm really looking forward to is winter. I'm dying to see this gorgeous landscape covered in snow."

"Wait till you're out there painting with your hand frozen to the brush," Malik comments.

"Wait until your rear end fuses to a chair," Amber tells him.

I've been getting to know Ms. Dunleavy. Malik calls me a traitor, and even the girls have a hard time seeing past her role in the early days of Project Osiris. Sure, she did that, but she's also the one shielding us from the questions that might come from police and other authorities about who we are and where we came from. Her goal is to protect us from all that until we're old enough to start college—when it won't make so much difference that our origins aren't the same as everyone else's.

It's the first time anyone has come up with a plan that ends with us having real lives.

Ms. Dunleavy also hired a firm of private investigators to search for what's left of Project Osiris. So far, they've come up empty. The town of Serenity is just as deserted as it was when we last saw it, and the inhabitants seem to have disappeared off the face of the earth. None of the people we mention—Osiris researchers or their kids—register hits in internet searches. We can't follow up on the Purple People Eaters because we don't know their real names, except for Bryan Delaney, who was married to our water polo coach.

And the only thing the detectives turn up on him is that his wife left him. Good for you, Mrs. Delaney.

The one name that generates a blizzard of activity is C. J. Rackoff, who broke out of prison in Texas. This is hardly news to us; we were the ones who sprung him. Still, an escaped convict is a pretty big deal. A massive manhunt has yet to turn up any sign of him. It only underscores the feeling that everything from our past has vanished.

Tamara Dunleavy never married or had kids. So as her clone, I'm the closest thing to a son she's got. We get along pretty well, which makes sense, considering we have the same DNA. It's weird to think that I'm identical to someone who's so much older than me, and a girl. When I look at her—gray hair, crow's feet, female—it's impossible to see myself.

But it's true. She had samples of our DNA tested. She shows me the report: except for the chromosomes that determine gender, we're a perfect match.

"I never really doubted it," she admits. "Felix may have been extreme, but his science was always top-notch."

I wince. For 99 percent of my life, I called that guy Dad. It's so recent that I was living in his house, dusting the framed photo of my poor dead mother, who never existed.

"I still think about him all the time," I confess. "Even a lousy parent is better than no parent at all. And believe me, he was a lousy parent, even without the Osiris part of it."

Ms. Dunleavy looks away. "I have to live with the role I played in what Felix did. But I can't help thinking that if there had been no Project Osiris, there would be no you, Eli."

"Could be you just like hanging out with yourself," I suggest, only half joking.

She laughs. "You're not me."

Maybe not, but when she watches me on a computer, it has to feel as if she's looking in a mirror. She gives me the odd pointer, but mostly, I can find my own way. I started out on Serenity's fake internet, and during our months on the run, I had to be satisfied with a few minutes online here and there. So when I get to Ms. Dunleavy's house, which is equipped with state-of-the-art technology and the fastest, highest-quality internet anywhere, I'm like a kid in a candy store. After more than thirteen years in a bubble, with Project Osiris deciding what I'm allowed to know, suddenly I've got the entire world at my fingertips. I read newspapers, watch videos, immerse myself in virtual reality simulations, explore, explore, explore.

With Ms. Dunleavy's help, I've designed an internet bot to scour every media outlet on the planet for the appearance together of two keywords: *criminal* and *DNA*. One morning, the program spits out a small article from page 19 of the *Manchester Guardian*:

DNA REVEALS AMERICAN CRIMINAL IN RESORT ROBBERY

WEST CAY, BAHAMAS: An investigation into a string of hotel room robberies on this idyllic island has led to a baffling mystery. Police arrested a maintenance employee on suspicion of a series of break-ins at the vast Poseidon Resort and Water Park here. Although no fingerprints were found at any of the crime scenes, police were able to extract a DNA sample from the root of a hair follicle in one of the rooms. The suspect confessed to the robberies before it was determined that his DNA did not match the specimen on the follicle.

Since the police had their man, they concluded that the hair must have come from a guest staying in the room.

Case closed—until the test result came back from the DNA lab. The specimen was a perfect match for Farouk al Fayed, a citizen of the United States. However, al Fayed, 61, could not possibly have visited Poseidon. He is currently serving twelve consecutive life sentences in a Minnesota prison for a series of kidnappings. He has not been a free man since 1994.

Scientists assert that it is impossible for even close relatives to present a genetic match of this exactitude. "Only identical twins can have identical DNA," a lab representative confirmed.

Yet Farouk al Fayed has no twin. In fact, he has no siblings at all.

The question remains: How did a hair follicle from a convicted felon

who's been jailed since 1994 make it
to an oceanfront mega-resort that was
constructed in 2009? . . .

It's like the temperature drops thirty degrees and I'm freezing and sweating at the same time. Farouk al Fayed—I've seen that name before. It was on a list with Gus Alabaster, Mickey Seven, Yvonne-Marie Delacroix, C. J. Rackoff, and the other criminal masterminds chosen to participate in Project Osiris.

And that means he wouldn't need an identical twin to get his DNA to a hotel room in the Bahamas. There's another way—a way that cops on some vacation island wouldn't think of in a million years.

I dash out the door and down the hall, into the nearest bathroom. I'm doubled over the sink, splashing cold water on my face when Malik bursts in.

"Whoa! What gives, Frieden? You look like you're about to keel over."

I have to blink to get the two images of him to come together. "Malik—" I croak, almost as if speaking my incredible discovery aloud will make it untrue, "I think I've found Project Osiris."

15

TORI PRITEL

Ms. Dunleavy squints at the article on the laptop in front of her. "Farouk al Fayed. Yes, he was one of them. Terrible man—the brains of an international kidnapping ring. I never met him. It was Felix who went to recruit him."

We're gathered around the tech billionaire in her luxurious office. Eli—brilliant Eli! Only he could see evidence of Project Osiris in that innocent headline in the *Manchester Guardian*. He didn't have much trouble convincing us of the importance of his discovery. But would Ms. Dunleavy believe it?

"Well, he can't be in the Bahamas because he's been in jail for more than twenty years," Eli points out. "There's only one other person with exactly that DNA—the Serenity

Kid who was cloned from him—Freddie Cinta."

Ms. Dunleavy looks skeptical. "Do you honestly expect me to believe that with his life's work crumbling around him, Felix decided to take Project Osiris on a vacation?"

"Not a vacation," I insist. "Don't you see? They're hiding out there!"

"At a water park resort?"

"It's the perfect place," I reason. "It's one of the biggest resorts in the world. And what do the guests look like? Parents and their kids. All they have to do to blend in is go to the beach, ride the waterslides, play with the dolphins, and have a great time."

"Figures," Malik puts in bitterly. "Thirteen years in Happy Valley and I never got past the third tumbleweed on the left. But the minute I'm gone, they take the whole place to an island paradise."

I know what he means. I used to *beg* my parents to take me on a trip to visit the great art museums of Europe. The answer was always no. Even though the real reason was obviously the Osiris experiment, the thought of the whole lot of them at some amazing resort bothers me.

Ms. Dunleavy makes a face. "It doesn't sound like the Felix Hammerstrom I remember."

"It's exactly him," Eli says grimly. "All smiles on the surface, but cold and calculating underneath it."

"What's so calculating about a vacation resort?" she asks, still bewildered.

"He set up shop in the middle of nowhere, surrounded on all sides by eighty miles of desert," Amber supplies. "This is his Plan B—an island, surrounded by ocean, so no one can get away like we did."

"And," I add, hoping I'm not thinking too much like Yvonne-Marie Delacroix, "if the FBI tries to arrest him for human cloning, they can't touch him because he's in a foreign country."

"It adds up," Eli concludes. "Serenity's a ghost town. After chasing us all over the country, no one's come after us since Texas. It's Hammerstrom's new strategy. He got worried that somebody might believe our clone story and took Osiris underground."

Ms. Dunleavy doesn't sound convinced. "The island police must be mistaken about the DNA. They're in a tiny jurisdiction without the kind of lab resources we have here in the US."

"DNA doesn't lie," Eli counters. "We're living proof of that."

Our billionaire hostess thinks about it for what seems like an eternity. Finally, she comes to a decision. "I'll send a pair of private investigators down to West Cay to look around. Let's test this theory of yours."

"And if we're right?" Amber demands eagerly.

Ms. Dunleavy sits back, arms folded. "We'll cross that bridge when we come to it."

The waiting isn't easy. When you're running for your life, you don't worry about the past. Your focus is the present— surviving the next few hours, the next few minutes, some-times the next few seconds. Of all the comforts that go along with living on a billionaire's estate, this is the one we least expect: the weird luxury of stressing over who might or might not be hiding on that island in the Bahamas.

They're more than just the personnel of Project Osiris. They're the parents who raised us, who loved us in their way; the Purples who kept us in line, and always just a lit-tle off balance; the kids we grew up with, including other clones who are still completely in the dark about who and what they really are.

On the third day after her investigators left for West Cay, Ms. Dunleavy strides into the kitchen where we're having dinner, her immaculate white sneakers silent on the granite tiles.

"Leave us, please," she says, and all her staff scramble out. She's always nice to us—motherly, even. But every now and then we catch a glimpse of her former life as a CEO, a tiger in the boardroom of VistaNet.

All business, she switches on the monitor against the wall. It glows to life with the message:

INVESTIGATION REPORT

POSEIDON RESORT AND WATER PARK

WEST CAY, BAHAMAS

"You found them?" Eli asks eagerly.

Ms. Dunleavy taps the tablet in her hand and a photograph appears on the big screen. Brilliant blue sky, palm trees, white sand, turquoise water. The composition's not great—the angle too high and the people off-center.

But that's not what causes my heart to leap into my throat.

"Steve!" I breathe.

Steve is what I used to call my dad. The surge of emotion is so raw that it's all I can do to hold back tears. One look at him and I'm six years old again, and he's hugging me and stroking my hair the way he did when I was upset. I was living a lie back then, but at least I was happy.

"Do you recognize these two?" Ms. Dunleavy prompts.

No one answers. The others are watching me, gauging my reaction. Malik is too much of a tough guy to admit he misses his Serenity parents; Amber is so angry that it overpowers any other feelings she might have. Eli was raised by Felix Hammerstrom himself, so it's easier for him to walk away. My cheeks are hot with shame. I'm the only one who can be shattered by a picture of a man who lied to me for more than twelve years.

"You okay, Tori?" Amber asks.

"I am," I reply shakily. And for some reason, saying it aloud makes it true. I turn to Ms. Dunleavy. "That's Steve Pritel, my Serenity father, and the boy is Robbie Miers, another one of the clones."

Ms. Dunleavy nods. "You kids were right. I don't know why I'm surprised. I of all people should understand how smart and resourceful you can be. Take a look at some of these other pictures."

One by one, the images appear before us—quickly at first, but when Ms. Dunleavy sees the emotional impact the photographs are having, she slows down. We hate Project Osiris, but that doesn't change the fact that, until very recently, it was our whole world—the same handful of people. It's our enemy, but it will never stop being part of us.

There they are, our fellow clones and their Serenity parents. Ben Stastny, his long hair blowing straight out behind him as he rides a wave runner; Penelope Sonas trying (and failing) to get herself upright on water skis; Aldwin Wo on an inner tube, passing through artificial rapids on a lazy river. All of them—Freddie Cinta of the famous hair follicle. Margaret Rauha.

"They seem—happy." It feels bittersweet to speak the words.

"Why wouldn't they be?" Malik retorts. "They grew up in the same one-horse dump we did. Look at that resort! It's like it's impossible *not* to have fun."

Amber's brow darkens. "That's not it. They're happy because they don't *know*."

It's as if the temperature in the kitchen suddenly drops fifty degrees. Robbie, Ben, Aldwin, Freddie, Penelope, and Margaret are just like us. And while fighting for our own future, we never gave much thought to what would happen to them.

"What kind of people are we?" I whisper.

"You know that as well as I do," Malik replies darkly.

"We're criminal masterminds. And so are they. They would have been just as selfish if our places were switched."

"You're being too hard on yourselves," Ms. Dunleavy cuts in. "You were fighting for your lives and freedom every minute."

We identify all our parents and several Purple People Eaters (they're harder to recognize in Bermuda shorts and bathing suits instead of their usual paramilitary gear). The sight of C. J. Rackoff in a Hawaiian shirt makes my stomach hurt. The only reason that terrible con man isn't in prison is that *we* broke him out. His clone, Hector, is in the next picture. Malik practically melts into his chair at the sight of his former best friend who stabbed us in the back.

We take note of some important absences. More than half the kids in Serenity weren't clones; they were the natural children of Osiris researchers. None of those families seem to be in West Cay.

"My investigators estimate there are between forty and fifty Osiris people at Poseidon," Ms. Dunleavy tells us. "Felix's inner circle, probably. He always talked about how only the most devoted researchers could be chosen to act as parents of the newborn subjects."

I cringe. Not devoted to *us*, to *the experiment*.

The last photograph appears on the screen. The four

of us gasp involuntarily. It's Felix Hammerstrom, his near-black eyes staring at the camera as if he can spot us, pinpoint our location, and dispatch a helicopter full of Purples to Wyoming to scoop us up. He's standing in front of an aquarium tall and wide enough to fill a wall three stories high. An enormous manta ray hangs in the water behind him. Below it swims a sand tiger shark easily ten feet long.

Between the shark and the former mayor of Serenity, New Mexico, it's hard to tell which is the more dangerous predator.

"Same old Felix," Ms. Dunleavy comments with a wan chuckle. "He's a little older, but I have to say he's barely changed. All the arrogance is still there, the belief that he knows what's best for everyone."

"Try growing up with the guy," Eli says bitterly.

Amber is impatient. "So that's it. We know where they are. What happens now? We call the cops, right?"

Our hostess mulls it over. "The problem is *which* cops do we call? West Cay is part of the Bahamas. American authorities have no jurisdiction there."

"What about the island police?" I ask. "Or the Bahamas government?"

"Assuming we could convince foreign officials that Project Osiris really exists, then what? They're not going to arrest upward of forty US citizens for something that sounds like the plot of a horror movie."

"So we just do *nothing*?" Malik demands.

"Of course not," Ms. Dunleavy replies. "I propose that I get in touch with Felix and—"

The four of us all start babbling at the same time, so our protest ends up nothing but noise.

"Let me finish," she persists. "I understand Felix is a monster to you, and I admit his methods are extreme. But he's a highly intelligent man who must recognize when he's out of options."

Eli is distraught. "And you think, what? That he'll just let you take the other clones because you ask him nicely?"

"No," Ms. Dunleavy admits. "But I'm going to convince him that Osiris is over, and there's no reason for him to hang on to those other children. And in exchange for their release, I'll pay him enough money that he'll have no financial worries for the rest of his life."

Amber is furious. "Just because they're clones doesn't mean they aren't people! You can't buy and sell people!"

"Felix considers this his life's work," our hostess argues. "He's not going to give it up until he knows that he's settled for the rest of his days."

"Like he deserves to get rich," Malik broods.

"No, he doesn't," Ms. Dunleavy agrees. "But he's got what we want, and he's not going to hand it over if we offer him what he deserves—which is a long prison sentence."

"I know what this is really about," Amber chimes in. "You won't call the cops on Hammerstrom because he knows about your hacker past!"

"Amber—" I begin warily. My best friend's face is red and getting redder.

"Well, it's true, isn't it? And all this money is nothing but a bribe to get him to shut up about it!"

"Not smart, Laska," Malik says. "Think about whose house this is."

"You're right," Ms. Dunleavy concedes. "I've done some bad things, and maybe I deserve to pay for that. But if I'm in prison, who's going to make this deal with Felix? Who's going to take in the new kids and protect them from the questions of the world, the way I'm doing with you?"

"And we're grateful," Eli assures her. "Honestly. But you can't talk to Hammerstrom—and it isn't because you'd be making a deal with the devil. The real problem is you'd be tipping him off that we're onto him. And he could take those kids and disappear. West Cay isn't the only island in the world, you know."

She's unmoved. "I think I know a little more about

the way things work than four kids who, up until a few weeks ago, lived incredibly sheltered lives. The money I'd be offering Felix—"

"He doesn't need money," Eli interrupts. "He's got Rackoff bankrolling him now. And if Osiris goes underground again, we'll never find them. It was a total fluke that we found them this time!"

Malik has a suggestion. "You've got two guys at Poseidon already. Why don't you send a few more in your plane, round up the kids, and fly them back here?"

Ms. Dunleavy is appalled. "That's kidnapping!"

"Suddenly we're worried about breaking laws?" Amber explodes. "Kidnapping is nothing compared with what was done to us and those innocent kids! Any way you get them out has to be better than leaving them there!"

"I agree." I put a hand on her shaking shoulder. This is no Mickey Seven overreaction. I'm with Amber 100 percent.

A stony hardness sets in our hostess's eyes. We're facing Tamara Dunleavy, CEO, again. An executive decision has been made, and no force in the universe is going to change it.

"I know you think you're right, but in this case, you're not. I'm going to consult with my lawyers and then reach out to Felix. You'll just have to trust me."

We stare at her. She rescued us. She's totally on our side—our only chance at a real life.

But we have to remember who else she is: the cofounder of Project Osiris.

She's been wrong before.

16

AMBER LASKA

I storm into the suite I share with Tori, slamming the door behind me. My latest list is right where I left it, on the nightstand next to my bed.

THINGS TO DO TODAY (UNPRIORITIZED)
- Running (5.5 miles)
- Swimming (60 lengths)
- Piano practice (try antique harpsichord) . . .

It's like it's mocking me. I snatch up a pen and cross everything out with such viciousness that the point tears through the paper, damaging the polished wood tabletop underneath it.

I don't stop. Unprioritized? I'll prioritize it. Hiking,

ballet, bird-watching—where do those things rate in a world where kids just like me are in the hands of Project Osiris and nobody is doing anything about it? Compared with that, the items on my list should be so low that they'd need booster rockets to reach the bottom of the page. Am I that small-minded? That shallow? The evidence is right here in front of me.

The door opens. "Amber, stop!" Tori says in alarm. "You're ruining it!"

"Nothing deserves to be ruined more than this list!"

"Not the list," she exclaims. "The nightstand!"

I pick up the shredded paper to reveal the scratched tabletop. "I don't care about the stupid nightstand!" Actually, I do feel kind of bad about that, but it's so much less important than everything else that it's hard to get worked up about it. "I'm not a good person, Tori. I thought I was, but I'm not."

"We obviously all have weird feelings about our DNA—"

"It has nothing to do with Mickey Seven!" I wave the tattered page at her. "I spend my whole life obsessing over me, me, me! And Penelope—Margaret—Robbie—"

"Maybe Ms. Dunleavy knows what she's doing," Tori suggests dubiously.

"By telling Felix Hammerstrom we know where he is? You're supposed to be the master of strategy!"

"It does kind of seem like giving up the one advantage we have," she admits.

There's a knock at the door, and Malik and Eli step into our room.

"We have to talk," Eli announces.

"We've talked enough," I say irritably.

"We can't let Ms. Dunleavy tip off Project Osiris," Eli goes on.

"How are we going to stop her?" Tori counters. "It's not like we can tie her to a chair, or hit her over the head. She's got staff working here—security people."

Eli shuts the door. "We're not going to stop her. We're going to beat her to the punch."

"Spit it out, will you?" Malik snaps. "This crazy idiot thinks we can sneak down to West Cay and kidnap those six kids away from Osiris!"

Tori and I are stunned. It's so obvious. Why didn't we think of it? Actually, we *did* think of it, sort of. Malik tried to convince Ms. Dunleavy to use her own people to grab the others away. But when she refused, the next logical step would be to do it ourselves.

"Now you're talking!" I exclaim.

Malik glares at me. "Brilliant, Laska. We almost got killed, like, fifty times trying to escape Project Osiris. So it makes perfect sense to blow off the one person who helped us and airmail ourselves to the same mad scientists who created us in the first place. Yeah, that makes amazing sense."

"It would be really risky," Tori puts in. "You heard the report. There are between forty and fifty Osiris people at Poseidon."

"And that makes a difference?" I demand. "I don't care if there are fifty *thousand* Osiris people at Poseidon! I saw your faces in the kitchen! Those are the kids we grew up with! The only other people like us in the *world*! Maybe it's okay that we forgot them while our own lives were in danger. We can't forget them now."

"I said it'd be risky. I never said we shouldn't do it," Tori replies with determination.

"And you're supposed to be the big planner?" Malik rasps at her. "Would Yvonne-Marie Delacroix try to knock off a bank she knows it's impossible to rob?"

I stick out my jaw at him defiantly. "Maybe that's how she got caught. After all those crimes, she was finally doing something positive."

"The key word," he returns, "is *caught*. Don't you think I'd love to rescue Robbie and Aldwin and Margaret and the others? But that's not what would happen. We wouldn't be gaining *their* freedom; we'd be throwing *ours* away!"

"I'd rather be caught than live with myself knowing I could have helped and I didn't," I shoot back.

"I guess that's the difference between you and me," he says. "I'll live with myself just fine. Wasn't that supposed to be the point of all this—getting real lives? We fought *so hard* to have a future, and now you want to trash it? Well, be my guest, but don't expect me to climb aboard the Stupid Express with you. There are a lot of Tater Tots in the world. I intend to stick around to eat my share."

"Fine," I sigh. "We'll do it without you." When it comes to arguing with Malik, I can usually go on for hours. Suddenly, though, I haven't got the energy. Maybe it's an uphill climb we're facing. "Stay here with your Tater Tots. Eat yourself into a coma."

His face flashes red. "You have to be the most annoying person *ever*! All three of you—I'm surrounded by morons!"

"It's okay, Malik—" Eli begins.

"No, it isn't!" he rages. "Because now I'm going to have to go with you just to keep you nitwits from getting yourselves killed!" He glowers at me. "Thanks a lot, Laska!"

I feel my face twisting into a smile, which only enrages Malik further.

"Here's a practical question," ventures Tori. "West Cay is eighty miles off the coast of Florida. We're in Wyoming, on the other side of the continent. We've got no money, and one of the richest, most powerful women in the world doesn't want us to go. How are we going to get there?"

"Oh, no problem," Malik sneers. "Laska will put it on one of her to-do lists. You know, between the squat-thrusts and the organic brussels sprouts."

He's just being his usual self. But for some reason, as soon as he says it, I understand that we *will* get there. How? The same way we managed to break out of Serenity and elude the Purples and find Tamara Dunleavy and break Rackoff out of jail and crisscross the country and make our way to Ms. Dunleavy again.

We did it because we wanted to learn the truth about ourselves, because we wanted to get justice, because we wanted to have a chance to turn our fake lives into real ones. We did it because what choice did we have?

We have even less choice now. It's pure luck that we know exactly where Project Osiris and the Purples are holding our fellow clones. If we let this opportunity pass, we'll surely never get another one.

It's time to act.

17

ELI FRIEDEN

As a tech pioneer, Tamara Dunleavy made her fortune on the idea that almost everything can be done over the internet. TV, movies, music, and all forms of entertainment and information can be streamed. Machines can perform self-diagnostics and report problems directly to repair crews. Houses can communicate gas and electric meter readings. Tagged endangered species can be tracked. Cars can drive themselves. Sensors in human bodies can contact doctors *before* the patient ever becomes sick. VistaNet, her company, earned billions improving people's lives through the limitless potential of the web.

So it makes perfect sense that almost everything in Ms. Dunleavy's Jackson Hole compound runs on internet-based platforms—including the surveillance system that sends images from hidden cameras all around the vast house and property to a bank of TV monitors in the security office.

It's a good idea—until it isn't anymore.

You can't really blame Ms. Dunleavy for thinking it's safe. She wrote the computer code for it all personally, so she figured that the only hacker who could break into it would be her. It never occurred to her that nearly fourteen years ago, Felix Hammerstrom made an exact copy of her, only male. Or that I'd have a very good reason for needing to mess with her system now.

I feel kind of bad because Ms. Dunleavy's been so good to us—and even worse because I'm using one of her own computers to hack into her security system. But then all I have to do is think of the other clones to firm up my belief that what I'm doing is necessary.

And, as Malik puts it, "Big deal, you feel bad. I feel bad about being some kind of freak, and being raised by scientists instead of parents, and running for my life, and watching the only guy I'm really related to die right in front of me. Believe me, there's enough bad in all this to fill the Grand Canyon. Tamara Dunleavy can line up and take her lumps with everybody else."

Tori has mapped out the house and determined that we'll pass four security cameras between our rooms and the garage. Once I get past the firewall, my job is to replace those four feeds by replaying ten minutes from earlier in the night in an endless loop. That way, the security guard will never see us in the halls, on the stairs, at the side entrance, or in the garage.

Ms. Dunleavy goes to bed around eleven. I wait until midnight before starting the process. She's taught me a lot about her programming technique, which turns out to be helpful as I'm stabbing her in the back. Even so, it takes me two hours to gain control of the system and make the changes.

We tiptoe through the big house, peering fearfully around us for cameras Tori's scrutiny might have missed. Even as we let ourselves into the garage, we're half expecting the lights to blaze on and Ms. Dunleavy's armed guards to tackle us from behind.

Tori reads my mind. "It's fine. There's only one security guy at night, and he's in the control room, watching nothing on the monitors." She hesitates. "You know, this is the first real home we've had since we left Serenity."

Malik is impatient. "So we'll send her a postcard from Poseidon—'Having a wonderful time. Glad you're not here.'"

Actually, he's pretty antsy, and so am I. We hope we've

thought of everything, but we can't know for sure until we've passed through the gate with no alarms, no searchlights, and no running feet behind us.

As we scamper across the compound, the stars are as vivid and spectacular at night as the mountain scenery is by day. I tighten my grip on the strap of my backpack, which holds a single change of clothes and a laptop computer. I don't feel great about taking the laptop—Ms. Dunleavy's are all custom-built for extended battery life and the ability to pull internet from satellites. Just one more theft on my already guilty conscience. But if we're going to have any chance of succeeding in this crazy mission, we're going to need all the special talents we've inherited from the people we're cloned from. For better or for worse, mine are useless without a computer.

The garage is only two hundred yards away, but it seems a lot farther when you're expecting a tap on the shoulder any second. Yet as soon as we're inside, we're happy for every inch of distance from the house. The last thing we need is Ms. Dunleavy waking to the sound of a car engine.

When I head for the driver's-side door of the Bentley, Malik elbows me out of the way. "Nice try, Frieden. This car is my baby. I'm driving."

Amber sighs. "I wish we didn't have to steal it *again*."

Malik shoots her a dazzling smile. "If you're going to jack the same car twice, it might as well be awesome. Now buckle up."

The sound of the garage door opening is far too loud to suit me, but the Bentley purrs like a kitten. For all his bluster, Malik is very careful backing out and turning the car around. And then we're heading down the mountain toward town.

The girls and I are peering out the back window, and Malik's eyes are on the rearview mirror. All is quiet behind us. The car's clock gives the time as 2:42 a.m.

While Malik steers, I key our destination into the navigation system. It's not complicated. We're headed for Jackson Hole airport, more specifically, the 6:05 a.m. flight to Salt Lake City. From there, we'll catch a connection to West Cay and Poseidon. So at least the Bentley isn't going very far from home this time.

We already have our tickets, charged to Ms. Dunleavy's credit card. That has nothing to do with my hacking; it's the result of Tori's pickpocketing skills. I figure if Ms. Dunleavy's earning potential comes with her DNA, I should be able to pay her back someday. It won't make up for betraying her. But then again, if regrets were nickels, we'd all be richer than Ms. Dunleavy.

At least we're flying coach. Malik wanted to book us in first class.

"You guys are such losers! Having a Bentley means you travel in style!"

"We don't *have* a Bentley," Amber points out. "We just borrow one from time to time."

"And we're not proud of that," I add.

Ms. Dunleavy's compound is nestled amid rocky peaks, twenty miles outside Jackson. At three in the morning, the route is pitch-black and absolutely deserted. Only the car's state-of-the-art halogen headlights show us where the pavement ends, giving way to precipitous slopes and outright cliffs. Malik seems to be rethinking his decision to drive as he peers out the front windshield, eyes saucer-wide, terrified of missing a turn in the road, plunging all of us—not to mention his precious Bentley—to our deaths.

Eventually, though, the terrain flattens out, and we cross the rickety bridge over the Snake River. Even the town is dark and deserted as the car's navigation directs us through the streets. The only sign of light or life is coming from a rough-looking bar across from the long airport driveway. Several large motorcycles are parked outside, and a flickering neon sign declares it to be Boss Hawg's.

"I guess now we know who stays up late in Jackson Hole," Amber comments disapprovingly.

"Think about who you're cloned from before you look down on a few bikers," Malik tosses over his shoulder.

"I could say the same thing about you," she retorts.

The airport is tiny, but new and nice, all wood beams and glass. As we pull up in front of the terminal, we can see lights on and a couple of cleaning people inside. Otherwise the place is empty, which makes sense. We're nearly three hours early for the first flight of the day.

Malik turns off the car and gets out. "All right, let's go."

Amber points to the sign at the curb. "This is a no-parking zone."

Malik stares at her. "We stole a quarter-million-dollar car and you're worried about getting a *ticket*?"

In the end, we make him pull around into the lot. The last thing we want to do is call attention to ourselves—as if four kids driving a Bentley and traveling with no suitcases and no adults can ever blend into the background.

The one thing we do have now is ID. We have Ms. Dunleavy to thank for that. Part of the plan where we live with her is starting school in September. Her cover story is that she's raising four orphans. So she got us fake birth certificates and passports to show the principal when we register. We're hoping they'll get us past the security check-point when it's time to board our flight.

Once inside the airport, we find a bench in an incon-spicuous location and compare our cards. They have our real names and ages, and give different places of birth around Wyoming. The documents have even been arti-ficially distressed so they don't look too new. Tamara Dunleavy doesn't do anything halfway. Being a clone may be no fun, but at least I'm cloned from quality.

"Do you think these will be good enough to fool the TSA?" whispers Tori, casting a nervous glance in the direction of the checkpoint.

"They'd better," I reply grimly. "Remember, the flights are the easy part. It's when we arrive at Poseidon that things start to get hairy."

Malik tries to stretch out on the hard metal bench. "I hate waiting. Why does travel always have to be so boring?"

"I like boring," I insist. "If our lives could stay nice and boring it would be fine with me."

Tori sighs. "You sure dream big."

The time drags. Shortly after four, a couple of the ticket counters turn their lights on, and at four thirty, the TSA officers open the checkpoint. But there's no one for them to check—we're the only passengers in the airport so far.

"Where is everybody?" I mumble uneasily. Our whole plan is to pass through security in the middle of a crowd, when four kids traveling alone won't arouse any suspicion. "I bought our tickets just yesterday and the plane was practically full."

"Maybe people come at the last minute?" Amber muses.

I shrug helplessly. That's one of the disadvantages of our sheltered upbringing in Serenity. Except for Ms. Dunleavy's jet, none of us has ever been on a plane before. We just don't know.

The airport doors slide open to admit a stocky man striding urgently across the terminal. Amber emits a little gasp. It's Gavin, Ms. Dunleavy's nighttime security chief— the one who let us sneak out right under his nose because he was watching camera feeds of quiet halls, closed doors, and a garage that still had a Bentley in it.

Shocked, I grab at the others, who seem to have the same idea as I do—dragging ourselves into the only nearby cover—the men's bathroom. Somehow, we manage to scramble inside, tripping over each other's feet, and close the door behind us.

"What's he doing here?" Malik hisses, rounding on me. "You said the fake camera feeds would work!"

"Somebody must have checked on us," I reason. "Maybe Ms. Dunleavy's a light sleeper." I'm not, but everything doesn't have to come from DNA.

"How did she know to look for us here?" Malik demands.

"There aren't that many ways out of Jackson Hole," Tori reasons. "If she guessed we're going to Poseidon, the airport's a no-brainer."

I risk opening the door a crack. Gavin stands with the TSA personnel at the checkpoint. To get to our flight, we'll have to walk right past him.

I shut the door and give them the bad news. "Brace yourselves, you guys. We're not going to make that plane."

"But we can't just go back to Ms. Dunleavy and pretend nothing happened," Amber protests. "Now that she knows we're trying to get to Poseidon, she'll put security on us around the clock."

Tori has a suggestion. "Remember when Ms. Dunleavy first brought us up here? Her jet didn't fly into Jackson Hole. We landed at some other airport—"

"Driggs, Idaho," Amber supplies.

I've spent enough time on the run with Tori to predict where her methodical mind is going to take her next. "So if we can get ourselves *there*," I conclude, "we might be able to catch a different flight."

"Back to the Bentley!" Malik urges. "But what about Gavin?"

"Follow me," Tori orders.

Tori in the lead, we slip out of the bathroom, drop to the floor, and roll to a half wall that protects us from Gavin's view. Doubled over low, we scamper across the terminal, coming to a halt just short of the glass entrance doors.

"Uh-oh," Amber murmurs.

Outside in the parking lot, we can just make out the top of the Bentley's elegant profile. Right next to it stands another security man.

I swallow hard. So much has gone wrong already, and we haven't even left the city limits of Jackson.

"This way," whispers Tori.

We crawl on our hands and knees past the baggage claim and then get up and run between the closed car rental desks to a side entrance. From there, the woods are about forty yards away. It's not a sure thing, since we'll be in full view of the guy standing with the Bentley. But he's watching the airport, not the property around it. And anyway, it's not like we have much choice at this point.

One by one, we make the dash into the cover of the

trees. I go first, followed by Amber, Tori, and finally Malik. He's taller than the rest of us, and almost knocks himself silly on a low-hanging branch.

"You're bleeding!" Amber breathes.

"Really? How bad is it?" Malik reaches a hand to his brow and cowers at the sight of dark blood. "It's bad, right?"

All I can think of is the distance between us and Poseidon, which feels like it's growing. "If it's the worst thing that happens to you in the next couple of days, you're lucky."

"Easy for you to say, Frieden," Malik retorts. "It isn't *your* face!"

"How are we going to make it to that other airport?" I ask Tori.

She has no answer. "I only know that we can't stay here."

We jog through the woods, ducking under branches, sidestepping trees, and hurdling roots and underbrush. We're paralleling the airport property, keeping the main drive in sight. No new cars have arrived, which means Ms. Dunleavy hasn't called in any more security—or worse, the police. She doesn't want anyone looking into who we are any more than we do.

Ms. Dunleavy, who treated me like a son. And who I stabbed in the back.

Up ahead, the road beckons. We keep moving, not thinking too much about where we're going. Away from the airport is enough for now. There's zero traffic—after all, it isn't even five a.m. yet. So where's that music coming from?

Amber frowns. "Who plays heavy metal before dawn?"

That's when we see it: Boss Hawg's, the biker bar, sitting all alone at the edge of the road, practically in a ditch. Regardless of the hour, the joint is jumping.

And suddenly, Tori is smiling. She says one word:

"Transportation."

18

MALIK BRUDER

I figure little Miss Torific has lost her mind—until I see the motorcycles.

"Oh no you don't! Not those! No way!"

"You had no problem stealing a quarter-million-dollar Bentley," Frieden challenges.

"It's not the stealing that bothers me," I tell them. "It's the riding. And the crashing. And the dying."

Laska laughs out loud. "Wouldn't you know it? He's afraid of motorcycles."

I bristle. "I'm not afraid of motorcycles. I'm afraid of falling off motorcycles. I've lost enough blood for one night."

"Yeah, half a thimbleful," Amber shoots back. "You need a transfusion. Oh, wait—the only way to get to the hospital is by motorcycle."

"It's just like riding a bike," Tori reasons. "Only you don't have to pedal."

"And anyway," Frieden adds, "we can't stand here arguing about it. The sooner we get to the airport in Driggs, the sooner we can find a flight."

So those three—who accuse *me* of being a bully—basically bully me into doing it. We creep over to the roadhouse, keeping one eye on the front door of the bar. Most of the bikes have the keys still in them. I remember that from Gus's crew. The guys always left their keys in their cars, even when they were parked on the street overnight in front of the mansion. Nobody would be crazy enough to steal from Alabaster people. Payback would be a monster.

But *we're* crazy enough to steal from a motorcycle gang.

We choose two of the bikes and open the tire valves on all the others, jamming tiny pebbles against the stems so the air hisses out. Whatever keys we find Tori throws in the ditch. At this point, I'm so terrified that an army of enraged bikers is coming through the door to pound us all into hamburger, that I don't think twice about getting on the Harley behind Frieden.

I have to show him how to jump the engine. Luckily, a couple of Gus's guys had bikes, and I had a chance to watch them. We lurch forward for a second but lose momentum quickly, and the heavy machine starts to wobble. It's all we can do to get our feet down to keep it from rolling on top of us.

"Harder on the throttle!" I shout.

He's clueless. "Where's that?"

"The twisty doohickey on the handlebars!"

Tori must hear me, because she tears off down the road on the other bike, Amber on the seat behind her.

"Hang on!" Eli tosses over his shoulder. He revs the throttle as far as it will go.

The burst of acceleration is so huge that we practically do a wheelie. We exit Boss Hawg's at a thousand miles an hour and flash past Tori and Amber like they're standing still. I clamp my arms around Eli's midsection and hang on tight. The corner of the laptop in his backpack is poking into my stomach. I squeeze harder.

"Easy, Malik, you'll break my ribs!" he wheezes back at me.

I don't ease up. I can't. If I do, I'll go flying off the back of this thing and get run over by the girls, who are already fifty feet behind us.

The music in the roadhouse is pretty loud, but not loud enough to cover the roar of two motorcycles. The size of the guys who come pouring out of there would scare

Godzilla—or even Gus. I know this for sure, because they sure scare his clone.

"Faster, Frieden! Faster!" I holler in Eli's ear.

He twists the throttle on the handlebars and we shoot ahead. At that, the girls pass us on the inside. I risk a backward glance and instantly wish I hadn't. Three big bikes are coming up from the rear, gaining on us.

"What's going on? I thought their tires were flat!"

"I thought so too!" Another twist of the throttle and we're going even faster. Every bend in the road threatens to hurl me off the Harley. I sense last night's dinner rising.

Another curve, and I catch sight of our pursuers out of the corner of my eye. They're barely fifty feet behind. We're doing over eighty miles an hour, but there's no way we can expect to outrace experienced bikers. I can feel the vibrating heat of their engines crawling up my spine.

A meaty hand reaches for me—only a couple of feet away and closing. I think: *What a tragedy to survive Project Osiris only to be murdered by drunken bikers somewhere in Wyoming.*

Still hanging on with one arm, I pivot on the seat in a vain attempt to defend myself. Suddenly, the pursuing motorcycle begins to wobble and fall away behind us, my attacker's expression changing from fury to dismay.

"What's happening back there?" Eli bellows.

"It worked!" I crow, weak with relief. "Their tires are flat! They can't keep up with us anymore!"

I'm still pretty freaked out about falling off the motorcycle, but at least now nobody's chasing us. I consider suggesting that slowing down might be a good idea, but decide that putting distance between ourselves and Jackson Hole is an even better one. We may have slowed down the bikers, but Ms. Dunleavy's security people must still be searching for us somewhere.

The girls are dead ahead, ghostly pale in the glow of our headlight. After a few more minutes of riding, I'm even starting to get the hang of the Harley a little. The key is to lean whenever Eli leans as we take the curves. It'll never match the comfort and style of the Bentley, but at least I don't feel like I'm about to be launched into orbit with every bump in the road.

Just when I'm starting to relax a little, Frieden pulls even with the girls and motions them over to the side.

"What's the big idea?" I complain over the idling of the bikes. "No pit stops!"

Eli pulls the laptop out of his backpack. "We need to figure out where we're going."

Yeah, okay, I admit that would help. We set the computer

on the seat and huddle around the screen as he calls up a map.

The northwest corner of Wyoming isn't quite the one-horse whistle-stop Happy Valley is, but it has to come in a close second. If you're on pavement, chances are it's a straight shot to just about everywhere around. Frieden plots the route to Driggs and makes sure we all know it, in case the two bikes get separated.

He's just about to close the laptop when a notification sounds, and a pop-up window opens. Tamara Dunleavy is peering out at us, one angry CEO. "Eli—kids—listen to me—"

Frieden closes the pop-up. But as soon as it's gone, a new one appears, and she's ticked off at us from a slightly different angle. Eli puts his thumb over the webcam, blocking her from seeing where we are—not that she could pick up much beyond the fact that we're in the middle of nowhere in the pre-dawn gloom.

Ms. Dunleavy tries again, kinder this time. "I know you're only trying to help your fellow"—she hesitates—"the others who are like you—"

"Fellow clones?" Laska cuts her off. "Whose fault is it that there are any clones at all?"

Ms. Dunleavy flushes a little. But being rich means

never having to say you're sorry. "I can't change the past. But if you trust me, I can help the others."

"You're not going to help them," Tori accuses. "You're going to ruin it for them."

"No." The CEO is coming back.

All this is tearing Frieden in two. He's her clone, her flesh and blood, complete with the family hacker skills and the resemblance to the kid in California. Eli never had a mother, not even the fake Serenity kind. This old billionaire is the closest he's ever going to get to a real one.

"You've been fantastic," Eli manages. "But those kids at Poseidon—I wish I could explain it better. They're—*us*. We already abandoned them once. We can't let them down." He slams the laptop shut.

If there was a point where we could crawl home to Ms. Dunleavy and beg forgiveness, we just passed it. I miss the Tater Tots already.

The sky is beginning to lighten as we get back on the bikes heading for Driggs. Twenty minutes later, when we pull into the airport, it's full dawn.

We look around in dismay. The sign says *DRIGGS-REED MEMORIAL AIRPORT*, but it's nothing more than an open field, with a couple of hangars that look more like barns and a single dinky square building marked *TETON*

AVIATION CENTER. There's a handful of small planes scattered around the tarmac, and a grand total of two cars in the parking lot.

"Where's the ticket place?" I ask.

Nobody answers. Jackson Hole airport wasn't big, but it was pretty clear where you had to go to catch your flight. Here, there's nothing.

"Maybe that guy knows." Tori points across the gravel drive to a lanky young man dozing on a wooden bench in front of the one and only building. The peak of his baseball cap is pulled low, hiding most of his face, and his head rests on a battered canvas backpack.

We park the motorcycles and walk over.

Eli does the talking. "Uh—mister? Sorry to disturb you, but where do we go to buy tickets?"

The guy stirs, opens one eye, and then sits up to take us in. The name *Shanahan* is stitched onto the knapsack. "Where did you kids drop from?"

Tori takes over. "We need to get on the next flight. Is the ticket counter inside?"

Shanahan's reply is an elaborate yawn that lasts several seconds. He pulls a pair of round wire-rimmed glasses from his pocket and settles them on his nose. "Where are you trying to get to?"

Tori is reluctant to offer too many details. "Well, where does the next flight go?"

"Depends."

We stare at him.

"This is a private airfield, guys," Shanahan explains. "Mostly for rich ranchers and fat cats in the oil business. United Airlines couldn't find this place with a telescope. So if that's the kind of flight you're looking for, you're out of luck."

He must notice the look of horror on our four faces. We've stolen a Bentley and two motorcycles to get to an airport that isn't a real airport. The most important thing we've ever tried to do is circling the bowl. It's not good.

"Sorry," he adds.

"So why are you here?" I ask.

He yawns again. "Waiting to be chartered. Pete Shanahan, Shanahan Air Services. Hey, are you four in trouble? Running away from home or something?"

Eli cuts him off. "We want to hire you."

"What—a bunch of kids?"

"You've got a plane; we've got someplace to go," Eli tells him. "What more do you need to know?"

Shanahan's brow jumps all the way to his hairline. "I

need to know who's after you—and therefore me. I need to know what to tell the cops when they arrest me for kidnapping."

"We're eighteen," I pipe up.

He laughs in my face. "*You* could pass for sixteen—maybe. The others—uh-uh."

"We have money," Tori volunteers.

His eyes narrow. "How much?"

You know how guys like Torque are experts when it comes to pinpointing your weaknesses? Well, suddenly, I sense a little vulnerability in Shanahan. Young pilot, probably the low man on the totem pole at Driggs, struggling to get his business going. In a way, he's almost as desperate as we are. He needs *money*.

"Don't worry about that, hotshot," I bluster. "Just gas up your plane and let's rock and roll."

I'm doing my best to sound like Gus's crew, but in reality, there's a lot to worry about. The only reason we had money before was Ms. Dunleavy's credit card number. But we can't count on that anymore. She figured out we were going to Jackson Hole airport, which means surely she checked into how we bought our tickets. Besides that, we've got barely a hundred bucks between the four of us.

He frowns at me. "Where exactly are you kids going?"

"We'll let you know once we're up in the air," I assure him.

He shakes his head. "It doesn't work that way. I have to know how much fuel to take on. I have to submit a flight plan to the tower. Should I go on?"

"There's an island in the Bahamas called West Cay—" Eli begins.

"You're not serious!" He looks us over, one by one. "You're serious! So not only am I flying a bunch of kids; I'm flying them out of the country? When they lock me up, they'll throw away the key!"

"How much?" probes Tori.

Shanahan's flustered. "You're talking thousands of miles! Plus hazard pay for the risk I'll be taking—twenty thousand."

I actually feel my jaw dropping open.

"Dollars?" Laska gapes in amazement.

We've learned a lot since escaping Happy Valley, but I guess we're still kind of clueless about what things cost in the real world. So much for chartering a plane for our piddly hundred bucks.

But Eli just says, "Done."

He unzips his backpack, and I swear the girls and I are

gawking at him as if he's about to pull out fistfuls of cash. But no, it's the laptop. He flips it open and pounds the keyboard. "I'll need your bank account number. I'll transfer the money in, and you can check on your phone to make sure it's there."

I'm positive he's blowing smoke to fool the guy, but when I look over his shoulder, the computer is going crazy. It's like sign-in screens for a million different websites are flashing all over the place, and passwords are magically appearing to fill them in. Next thing I know, the monitor is spitting out columns of numbers—big numbers. I read the name at the top—DUNLEAVY, TAMARA—and it hits me. Frieden has found a way to hack into *her* bank account to use *her* money to help us escape from *her*. It makes perfect sense. Who has a better chance of penetrating her cyber defenses than her own clone, whose brain is made up of her DNA, cell by cell?

I've got a little DNA of my own, and it has a suggestion. "Give him half."

"Half?" Shanahan repeats.

"Half now," I explain. "You get the other half when we land in West Cay."

Eli nods and hits the return button.

There's a beep, and a message appears: TRANSAC-TION COMPLETE.

"Check," Eli prompts Shanahan.

The pilot taps away at his phone for a while, and looks up in astonishment as he sees the brand-new deposit in his account. Believe me, he isn't half as amazed as I am. If poor Gus had realized it was this easy to get your hands on big money, he never would have wasted his life shaking down small-time storekeepers.

"Let's get Brutus," Shanahan says finally.

Brutus turns out to be his plane, not a guy. The only aircraft we've ever been on is Ms. Dunleavy's Gulfstream jet. Brutus is a big letdown. It—he?—is a six-seat propeller job that has seen better days. Or maybe it hasn't. Maybe Brutus was this crummy straight off the assembly line.

Riding in Brutus is like putting your head in a blender and setting it on liquefy. The floor shakes, the seats shake, the bulkheads shake, and the wings shudder as if they're about to fall off. But you don't worry about crashing. Between the nausea and the scrambled brains, you can't string two thoughts together.

"You get used to the vibration!" Shanahan shouts over the racket of the propellers.

I'll bet you don't.

It's a miserable flight. Did I say flight? How about flight*s*—plural? This fantastic piece of aeronautic engineering can't make it all the way across the country in one jump. Brutus has to stop and refuel every time the wind blows—once in Topeka, Kansas, and once in Meridian, Mississippi. Actually those stops are the only things keeping me going. Just having my feet on something that isn't shaking and roaring for a few minutes is a good trade-off for any delay in our trip. This isn't worth twenty thousand dollars—not even somebody else's twenty thousand dollars. It isn't worth twenty cents.

We eat vending machine pretzels, the only thing our sickened stomachs can keep down.

"Aren't you guys hungry?" mumbles Shanahan, chowing down on an enormous hero sandwich, gripped in oil-stained hands.

On top of it all, the trip takes forever. Brutus isn't just the lousiest plane that was ever built; it's also the slowest. We've been on the go for more than twelve hours when the land just sort of stops. Beyond it, stretching as far as the horizon in all directions, is water.

I thought I was too nauseated to care, but I've never seen anything like it before. "Is that the *ocean*?"

"First time?" Shanahan calls over his shoulder.

"It's *beautiful*!" Tori exclaims in awe. "The color! The texture!"

I swear if she turns this into an art lesson, she's going out the cargo bay.

"Didn't you guys see it in California?" asks Amber.

Eli shakes his head. "We went straight to Atomic Studios. There wasn't any time for sightseeing."

During this conversation, Brutus executes a wide, banking U-turn. All at once, the land is ahead of us instead of behind.

"Hey!" I shout to our pilot. "Why are we going back?"

He pivots in his chair. "Bad news, you guys. I just heard from the tower in West Cay. Our clearance to land has been revoked."

"What?" I choke. "Why?"

He shrugs. "You'd know better than me."

"How would *we* know?" Eli demands.

"Someone doesn't want you kids to get to the Bahamas," Shanahan explains. "Someone with a lot of clout."

And it hits us. Ms. Dunleavy. Who has more clout than a billionaire? We escaped her and her people in Jackson Hole, but she always knew what our final destination had to be. She couldn't call the cops on us—not without having to answer a lot of uncomfortable questions about our connection to Project Osiris and her connection to us. So she did the next best thing: she used her wealth and her reach to keep us from making it to Poseidon.

"That's your problem, man!" I shout at the pilot. "You took our money to fly us to West Cay! If you want the other half, you'd better get us there!"

Frieden does me one better. "I can take back the ten thousand you already have too. You saw how easy it was."

"You don't understand," Shanahan pleads. "If I touch down on that island, I could lose my license. I could be arrested. Brutus could be impounded."

"Also your problem," I shoot back.

"It's kind of our problem too," Tori muses. "Ms. Dunleavy already has two investigators on West Cay. If we land, they'll be at the airport waiting for us."

Laska's face is reddening. "We have to get there. I don't care how."

"I never should have agreed to take you kids," Shanahan laments. "Not for any money. Now I'm on the wrong side of the country with no place to land, and I have no choice but to take you home to your parents."

"Then you're off the hook," I growl. "We've got no home. And no parents either."

He stares at me.

"We're not going back to Wyoming," Amber says with deadly certainty.

"Well, make up your mind, guys," the pilot warns. "We can't just circle up here. Our fuel won't last forever."

Frieden points straight down. "What's this place?"

"Florida—north of Fort Lauderdale."

"We'll get off here," Eli decides.

"I know a private airstrip," Shanahan tells us. "Used to be a hangar for the Goodyear Blimp."

I have no idea what that is, but we have a more pressing problem. "What good is being here?" I demand. "There's still a lot of ocean between Florida and the Bahamas! How are we supposed to get there?"

"In one of those," Eli replies.

As the plane banks, we catch sight of the expanse of water. There's the beach and, way offshore, several sleek shapes moving through the blue, leaving white wakes behind them.

Boats.

19

TORI PRITEL

If you ever want to be looked at like you're crazy, use a laptop to call a taxi to pick you up at an abandoned blimp base.

By the time the cab jounces across the broken parking lot, Shanahan and Brutus have flown off into the sunset and we're draped across concrete benches in the long shadow of the hangar. Bone weary, Malik and Amber are out cold and snoring. The only reason why Eli and I are still upright is we're leaning against each other. But neither of us has the energy to talk. We haven't slept in more than a day and a half. And our real mission (the hard part) hasn't even started yet.

"How did you kids get here?" the driver asks in amazement, startling Amber awake.

"It's a long story," Eli tells him. "We need to get to the nearest marina."

Amber slaps Malik on the side of the head, and he sits up with a start. "I'll take a second helping of Tater Tots—" he murmurs, still half in a dream. Then his eyes open and he takes in his surroundings with a disappointed, "Oh."

The driver shakes his head with a mixture of disapproval and admiration. "You party animals. You get younger every year."

The motion of the taxi brings Malik the rest of the way back to life. (At least he's alert enough for complaining.) "I can't believe you paid that crook Shanahan," he mutters to Eli. "Even after he flew us to the wrong place."

"I didn't pay him," Eli defends himself. "I just let him keep the money he already has. What choice did I have? The online account has been frozen. That means Ms. Dunleavy knows we hacked into her bank."

"Another bonehead move by you," Malik accuses. "Why didn't you transfer out a few mil for us while you were in there? She never would have missed it. That's chump change to a billionaire."

"Because we're not our DNA," Amber says staunchly.

"Frieden hacking into bank accounts is *exactly* his

DNA," Malik retorts. "And how about the Bentley and those two motorcycles?"

"That's not *my* DNA," Amber reminds him.

"Okay, so we haven't blown anything up. But the day's not over yet."

"Quiet, you guys." I point to the driver and drop my voice. "The main thing is no more bank transfers." We have to be aware of our changing situation if we're going to have any chance of putting together a plan to get to West Cay. The odds are already stacked against us. "That means the only money we have left is what's jammed in our pockets. And that's not much."

"So how are we going to charter a boat to the Bahamas?" Malik asks in dismay.

"We're not," Eli replies evenly. "We're going to steal a boat and sail it there ourselves."

Amber closes her eyes. "More stealing."

"How are we supposed to find the Bahamas?" Malik demands. "We're not sailors. We grew up in New Mexico."

Eli pats his backpack. "The laptop has built-in GPS. I disabled it so Ms. Dunleavy couldn't track us. But by the time we're in the water, it'll be too late for her to catch up."

"You said *in* the water," Malik grumbles. "I hope you meant *on* the water."

It's almost dark when we get to the marina, and the taxi drives off with a substantial amount of our dwindling money. I know this isn't the time to be thinking like an artist, but this little harbor is an amazing place. The boats are bobbing gently, and the ocean is lapping at the dock. The lights of the marina are reflected in the water, and the just-risen moon is huge on the horizon. If you live near the sea, scenes like this are probably nothing special. But to me it's so beautiful and unique that the urge to paint it is almost an ache.

For a fleeting moment, I actually long for my house in Serenity, with its attic studio—*so* not a possibility, obviously. Anyway, I'll be turning my powers of observation on this place in a different way, looking for a good boat to steal. It isn't very artistic, but it's what we need right now. I wonder if Yvonne-Marie Delacroix had artistic talent too—before necessity turned her into a bank robber.

Malik points to a seventy-foot yacht, gleaming white with dark tinted windows. "That one looks pretty good."

"Too flashy," I tell him. "We need something that isn't so noticeable."

Malik scowls. "I knew it. We're going to get a lousy boat."

"We're not going to get a floating Bentley, if that's what

you mean," Amber informs him. "The idea is to get there, not to get there in style."

The marina is quiet, but far from deserted. Some of the day cruisers are still coming in, and a couple of the yachts are hosting dinner parties. We decide to slip into a small diner a few blocks in from the water, both to feed ourselves and also to pass the time until conditions are better for a boat theft.

I never thought I'd be hungry again after an entire day of Brutus doing a number on my stomach. But the cooking smells in the restaurant remind us that we're all starving. We eat a lot, even Amber.

We hang out at the table until the place closes at nine thirty and make our way back to the marina. The light in the harbor master's office is out now; the dinner parties are disbanded and gone. A couple of people are hosing down the decks of their boats. Otherwise, we have the place to ourselves.

We select one of the outer docks and make our way along the wooden pier, browsing like shoppers. The outer ranks are mostly fishing boats—not very luxurious, but good-sized and, more important, sturdy. We're looking for something easy to steal, but mostly easy to drive and seaworthy.

We have no sailing experience, since none of us has ever been anywhere near a boat. Malik and Eli step aboard each craft, hoping to find helm controls similar to a car's. That way, they know they'll have half a chance of being able to drive.

"This one," Eli decides suddenly.

Malik wrinkles his nose. "It smells like fish."

"It's a fishing boat," Amber observes. "What do you expect it to smell like? Chanel Number Five?"

"It's perfect," I tell them. "Look at the name on the stern—*Gemini*. The twins. Identical twins have the same DNA, just like clones."

Malik looks disgusted. "Well, if the name has the right symbolism, how could we go wrong?"

"Look." Eli motions us aboard. "There's a standard steering wheel, and that lever must be the equivalent of a gas pedal."

"No key," Malik puts in.

"No problem," I say. "We can hot-wire it like a car." (Scary how quickly the thought comes to mind.) "We just need a flathead screwdriver. There must be a toolbox we can raid."

"I'm on it." Malik disappears into the stern. We hear him opening lockers and sorting through gear.

At the helm, I get down on my hands and knees and begin feeling for a panel we can pry open. I've already broken one fingernail when Amber hauls me back to my feet.

"I've almost got it—" My voice catches in my throat.

Not a dozen steps in front of us, one foot still on the top rung leading from below, stands a mountain of a fisherman, easily six foot three, with a long bushy beard and furious eyes under heavy brows. In his giant hands he wields a lethal-looking spear gun.

His voice matches his appearance—gruff and larger than life. "What are you kids doing here?"

What are we doing? That's pretty obvious, isn't it?

"We can explain," Eli manages.

No, we can't. Not really. But if it keeps the guy from shooting us, I'm all for it. The razor-sharp spear point catches a harbor light and winks at us.

"A little young for joyriders, aren't you?" He gestures toward us with the weapon. "We'll see what the cops have to say about that."

If we get arrested, the police won't release us until there are parents or adults to hand us over to. Then our fellow clones will be doomed to spend the rest of their lives under the thumb of Project Osiris.

Out of the gloom behind the fisherman, a metal toolbox swings up and around, catching him on the side of the head with a sickening thunk. He drops like a stone, revealing Malik behind him, pale-faced and wide-eyed. The spear gun hits the deck and goes off. The harpoon fires with a hissing sound, burying itself into the console between Eli's knee and mine. (Too close for comfort.)

Malik's voice sounds much higher than usual. "Is he dead?"

I shuffle forward and put my hand on the fallen giant's chest. There's a strong heartbeat and he's definitely breathing. "He's alive!" I exclaim in relief.

"Let's steal a different boat," Amber suggests shakily.

"With maybe a different guy down below?" Malik challenges. "And this one's got a bazooka? No, thanks!"

"He's right," Eli says, rubbing his knee. "At least here, there are no surprises."

"Because they already gave us a heart attack!" Malik rasps.

Amber indicates the fisherman. "What about him?"

"He's not coming with us, that's for sure," replies Eli confidently. "Let's get him onto the dock."

Of all the difficulties we've faced since learning the truth about Project Osiris, moving the unconscious giant might be the hardest. (A million tons feels like two million tons when it's dead weight.) It takes all four of us to drag him across the deck and heave him over the side to the dock. He hits the wooden planking so hard that we have to do another breathing check.

"We can't leave him here like this," Amber announces.

"He nearly turned you into a shish kebab," Malik reminds her. "He's lucky we don't throw him to the sharks."

"He's really hurt," she insists.

I weigh the situation—the fisherman's need for a doctor versus ours to head out to sea without attracting attention. "We'll radio the harbor master to send an ambulance," I decide. "But not until we're really far from shore. We can't take the risk that they'll send a police boat after us."

Amber looks daggers at me, and it's pretty obvious what she's thinking: *That's exactly what Yvonne-Marie Delacroix would say.*

Being offended is a luxury I can't afford. We've got a boat with—I check the fuel gauge—a full gas tank, and West Cay is only eighty miles away.

We don't have to hot-wire the engine. The keys are on a ring hanging from the fisherman's belt. It takes a few minutes for Eli to back away from the dock, since he's being extra careful. We go super slow, with no running lights, until we're at the mouth of the harbor. Then it's out into open sea.

We feel the difference in the waves almost immediately. Every swell is like the miniature hill of a roller coaster. Our boat goes up, over, and down before the ocean aims us into the next climb.

"I can't do eighty miles of this," Malik says, his face turning green. "I can't do eighty seconds of it."

By trial and error, Eli realizes that speeding up will send us cutting over the top of the waves, rather than descending into the trough of every single one. It's incredible how many things he's learned how to do without ever being taught. It's like he can troubleshoot the world the same way he troubleshoots a computer. In all the craziness, sometimes I forget how much I admire him.

When we can't see the land beyond a few twinkling lights, I use the ship-to-shore radio to sound the alarm about the unconscious fisherman. "Never mind who this is," I tell them when they ask my name. "Just get him. He's going to have a big headache." I cut the connection.

By this time, Eli has the laptop out, and we're navigating by GPS, which says we are five hours and forty-two minutes from our destination—Poseidon's yacht basin on West Cay, Bahamas.

20

MALIK BRUDER

When we lived in Serenity, we were never allowed to watch movies or TV shows where anything bad or scary happened. But here in the real world, I've heard there's this old classic called *Jaws* where a giant shark goes around eating people and even sinking boats to get at them.

I hope they don't have that kind of shark in this part of the ocean. Because if they do, we'll never see it coming. Frieden found some sailing blog on the internet that tells you to keep your lights off to maintain night sight. Now we've got a quarter-moon and a few stars peeking out from behind the clouds. That's it. I thought I knew what dark was, but this is almost like being dead.

I'm alone at the wheel. Eli and the girls are on the computer, which we're recharging at an outlet. They're studying up on Poseidon so we'll know what to expect when we get there.

"You guys are watching the GPS, right?" I call over. "I wouldn't want to crash into an island or anything like that."

"We're still on course," Eli confirms. "Our speed goes up and down, depending on the wave action, but I think we're making good time."

"What's the matter, Malik?" Amber adds. "I thought you liked driving."

"I like driving *Bentleys*. This is creeping me out. There's no road, and even if there was, I wouldn't be able to see it. I could be heading for Iceland and never know it."

"The GPS says you're not," Tori returns wearily.

My back is killing me. This chair is made from pure titanium and for a guy about eight times my size. So here I am, straining forward, peering out into nothing, squinting to see even less. My head aches. My stomach is queasy. I'm not technically seasick, but I'm definitely sick of the sea.

At last, Eli comes to spell me. "The girls are both asleep. You should try to get some shut-eye."

Great. He expects me to sleep with what we've got ahead of us. As horrible as this trip is, the worst part is what happens at the end of it—what we have to do when we reach our destination.

We've spent weeks putting ourselves through the shredder to get away from Project Osiris. And now we're doing the exact opposite—running toward them, basically serving ourselves up on a silver platter. I was nuts to agree to it. But how could I leave the others to go it alone? How could I abandon *Laska*, who—despite being a huge pain in the butt—probably saved my skin half a dozen times?

Besides, as much as I hate to admit it, they're right. When you're one of only eleven like you in the whole world, you owe those people your loyalty. You don't think of loyalty as part of criminal DNA, but that's something I learned from Gus and his crew. Lenny kept the organization running despite the fact that it looked like Gus would never get out of jail. Even the *dog*, Counselor, waited more than a hundred dog years for his master to be released. If a German shepherd can be that loyal, I can too.

Well, it isn't easy, because if Project Osiris gets its teeth into us one more time, we'll never taste freedom again. Dr. Bruder—my own ex-father—will be mixing the potion that'll drag us back to Happy Valley and convince us we like it. He and the other parents will have us on a pharmaceutical combo that will erase the past weeks from our memories and make us forget who and what we are.

Who can sleep while sailing into *that*?

"I suppose you expect me to have sweet dreams, too," I mutter under my breath.

Laska turns over on the padded bench. "Quiet, Malik. You're not the only one who's scared."

"I'm not scared." The lie doesn't convince Laska, who can always read my mind.

There are only two benches, so I make myself a bed out of life jackets and stretch out on the deck. There's nothing to use for a blanket, but that doesn't matter, because it's hot and muggy. We're used to New Mexico dry heat. This is different—heavier, sweatier. I don't sleep exactly, although I must doze off a couple of times. It's better than nothing. Sort of.

Then Eli calls for all hands on deck and we join him at the helm.

There it is, dead ahead, just like the GPS told us it would be. The island is still in shadow, but the resort features are lit up—the huge hotel towers designed as Poseidon's undersea palace, and the massive volcano, its seven water-slides glowing red like lava flows from the crater.

"Just like on their website," Tori breathes.

"Look at this place," Amber says with a disapproving scowl. "There are hungry people in the world, and Poseidon has money to spend on a fake volcano."

Typical Laska. The nicer something is, the more she finds a way to dump on it.

Frieden is all about the mission. "We did it, you guys. The other clones are out there somewhere. We just have to find them."

We switch off our running lights as we approach the island. We can see more now—beaches, lush tropical greenery, a harbor filled with luxury yachts that make the *Gemini* look like a beat-up bathtub toy. To my surprise, we veer away from Poseidon's boat basin and start to curl around the island's coast.

"Hey," I tell Frieden, "you missed the parking lot."

Tori provides the explanation. "This boat's our getaway," she says, squinting as she and Eli anxiously search the shoreline. "We need to keep it hidden so we can load the kids on it and take off."

At last we come to a stretch of undeveloped coast, with a narrow strip of sandy beach overgrown by tropical plants. Hibiscus and mangrove, Torific supplies. Like we're writing a travel guide. What matters is it's the perfect spot—far enough from the busy resort, and bushy enough to hide our boat.

Give Frieden credit—he actually seems halfway nautical as we maneuver closer to the trees.

"Get the anchor," he orders.

The girls can't budge the thing, so I go to the stern to show them how it's done. Okay, it weighs a ton, but I'm able to heave it up and even lift it over my head. "Now, this is called manly strength—" I brag, wishing my voice didn't sound so strained.

There's a loud scraping sound, and the *Gemini* tilts under my feet. The heavy anchor falls from my hands and takes a divot out of the deck, missing my foot by millimeters.

"What happened?" Amber shrills.

Eli turns a white face to us. "We hit something!"

"Speak for yourself," I hiss. "*You* hit something! It better not be a giant shark!"

Tori grabs a long spear-tipped pole, leans over the side, and plunges the point straight down into the water. When she pulls it up, the barb has snagged sandy seaweed.

"It's only a sandbar," she reports. "It's good news. We can walk ashore."

One by one, we climb down the swim ladder and step off into the shallows—which aren't as shallow as we hoped. We're soaked to our waists, but I suppose when you're risking everything trying to do the impossible, being wet and uncomfortable is the least of your worries.

We reach the beach, still under cover of vegetation, and make our way to the edge of the trees. The Poseidon property is laid out before our eyes.

"Wow," Eli whispers. "Those kids must think they're in heaven."

I know what he means. The clones were plucked out of Happy Valley, the most boring place on earth, and dropped in the middle of fantasyland. Everywhere you look there are pools, patios, waterfalls, fountains, playgrounds, gardens, rides, and slides. Miles of lazy river meander around the grounds, snaking between the hotel buildings, the amphitheaters, and the shops and food kiosks.

"Even in the dark, it's breathtaking!" Tori says in awe.

Leave it to her to obsess on the wrong thing. "It's *fun*, is what it is," I insist. "Wouldn't it be great if we could just, you know, hang out here a couple of days before we start the rescue?"

"No," Eli retorts firmly. "My luck, I'd go off the diving board and land in the water right next to Felix Hammerstrom."

"Your old man?" I shoot back. "He'd look pretty dumb swimming in his three-piece suit."

We continue through the maze of walkways and flowerbeds. Poseidon is completely deserted now, yet we can almost sense hundreds of people, maybe thousands, asleep in the hotels and condos. The clock on the dolphin pavilion gives the time as 4:28 a.m.

"Atlantic time," Eli explains when Tori glances at her watch in confusion. "That's three hours later than Wyoming."

The center of the resort is Poseidon's "palace," which hosts the main hotel and restaurants. I've never been inside a real palace, but I'm guessing this is what one looks like— everything shiny and fancy, with crystal chandeliers, and even more gold than in Gus's house. One entire wall of the lobby is a humongous fish tank stretching three stories high. And no piddly little goldfish in there either. They've got giant sawfish and sea tortoises and sharks and a lot of other stuff I can't even name. When the manta ray spreads itself out, it's bigger than a tarp that you could hide a truck under.

"Hey! Hey, you!"

We jump. We've yet to see a single soul at Poseidon, so we're not expecting it when one actually pops up. A uniformed security guard is striding toward us. "What are you kids doing out at this hour? Go back to your parents." Suddenly, he's looking down, and I realize that he's noticing the puddle that's expanding at our feet. We're still dripping wet from our wade ashore.

"You've been in the pools," he accuses. "You know the pools are closed now!"

What are we supposed to say? We can't very well deny it without explaining where the water really did come from.

"We're sorry," Tori says shamefaced. "We won't do it again. Please don't report us."

The guard's face softens. "We can let it go this one time. Return to your rooms immediately."

We hurry toward the exit, our drenched sneakers squishing on the granite floor.

We're almost out when a brassbound door opens and an elderly man steps out of the casino. The sound hits us immediately—ringing bells, cascading coins, and an assortment of groans and cheers. Unlike the rest of the resort, the casino is open twenty-four hours, and even now there are guests in there. I guess you're allowed to lose your money at four in the morning so long as it doesn't float out of your pocket while you're in the pool.

That's when we see him. Laska grabs my shoulder and squeezes so hard that it's all I can do to keep from screaming. There, sitting at one of the dice tables is a tall, lean man with impossibly broad shoulders. We don't know his real name. We always called him Major Nosehair, because—well, do I have to paint a picture?

He's a Purple People Eater.

21

TORI PRITEL

The sight of a Purple People Eater not sixty feet away from us changes everything. Before, we were walking around like tourists, gawking at the wonders of Poseidon. Now the wave pools and the waterfalls and even the volcano might as well not exist. All that matters is what we have to do.

As soon as we're away from the casino and back out on the grounds, I take charge. (I'm not sure why that always happens. In certain situations, where nobody else knows what to do, it's as clear to me as if I'm reading an instruction sheet.) "The first problem is our clothes."

"What's wrong with our clothes?" demands Malik. "Besides the fact that they're wet and gross."

"Nobody wears jeans to a water park," I explain. "We want to blend in with everybody else in this place. We need bathing suits so we'll look like all the other kids here."

"It's a good idea," Eli agrees. "Except we've got hardly any money left. And none of the shops are open till morning."

I lead them along one of the paths to the base of an elegant condo building ringed by outdoor terraces. As I expected, at least half of the units have bathing suits and T-shirts draped over deck chairs to dry.

"Swimwear department," I announce.

"If you're a monkey," Malik adds.

I am a monkey, and the three of them should know it by now. "Come on, give me a boost."

Eli and Malik hoist me up to the point where I can get a handhold on a second-floor balcony. I force away the image of Yvonne-Marie Delacroix climbing in the window of a bank as I swing a leg over the rail. Ah—a one-piece, a bikini, and—uh, oh. There must be a really massive dad in this room. Eli and Malik could both fit in those trunks together. I toss the girls' stuff down to the others.

"What if they're the wrong size?" Amber calls up. (Leave it to her to stress over a perfect fit.)

I whisper a reply. "We pride ourselves on our selection." I step back on the rail, grip the support bars of the balcony above and pull myself up. I clamber onto the third-floor terrace, only to find no suits up there. But next door there's a larger balcony, probably belonging to a suite. They've actually set up a wooden drying rack covered in suits and towels. Jackpot.

The problem is it's ten feet away—too far to jump. (I may be a monkey, but I'm not a bird.)

I scan my surroundings. There's a small window about halfway between the terraces, creating a hint of a ledge. It isn't much (maybe an inch and a half or two inches) but it should give me a temporary toehold. From there, I can jump to the other balcony.

I hear a triple gasp from below as I step out to the window ledge. I shift my weight forward, preparing to launch myself the rest of the way, when the door slides open on the balcony I just left. Out steps a young woman in a long silk robe, a glass of milk in her hand. At first, I'm positive she's seen me. But, no—she's looking straight out at the volcano, her eyes blinking with sleep.

Desperately, I try to sink behind the stucco of the façade, pressing my face into the window. I've got nothing to hold on to, so I push hard against the slight overhang with the heels of my hands, just to give me some stability. There I hang, the pounding of my heart threatening to launch me off the side of the building, praying that the woman goes back inside before it occurs to her to glance to the right.

Far below, on the ground, three horrified faces stare up at me. It's a sign of how quickly things can turn in an operation like this. Climbing is no big deal for me, but it only takes one tiny glitch to put my life in danger.

My bent knees are on fire and my shoulders ache from the effort of keeping myself wedged in position with my arms. How much longer can I stay like this?

Come on, lady, it's five o'clock in the morning! Go back to bed!

She makes the milk last, smacking her lips with every sip. Finally, she reenters the room, closing the slider behind her.

I leap for the next balcony. When my hands grasp the railing, they're so cramped up that I can't grip. But I manage to propel myself over it. I lie on the tiled floor for a few seconds, breathing hard with exhaustion and relief.

This time I don't worry about sizes or styles. I take everything on the drying rack and dump it over the side. I don't care if I have to wear a size nine hundred bathing suit. I'm done with climbing for the day. For good measure, I toss down three baseball caps that are hanging over a chair back. The more of our heads and faces we can cover, the better.

I descend very carefully, and when I make it to the

bottom, I get a big reception. I guess they're glad to see me in one piece.

"You're not the one who'd have to face the Purples if you got yourself killed!" Malik rants, his angry voice muted. (That's what passes for heartfelt concern coming from Gus Alabaster's DNA.)

Amber and I change in the bushes. The guys use the opposite end of the building. Eli, Malik, and I take the baseball caps. Amber's the safest to go hatless, since her hair is different from what the Serenity people will remember.

We stuff our clothes in a locker, but of course, the kiosk where the locks are given out won't be open for a few hours yet. Now we just need a place to lie low until the resort comes to life and we can start our clone hunting.

We stumble on a storage hut piled high with inflated inner tubes for the waterslides. Comfort-wise, it's a real find. Those things make amazing beds. Exhausted as we are, though, nobody sleeps. We're in the middle of the lion's den, and closing your eyes is a bad idea.

"The last time I wore a bathing suit was Serenity Day—the big water polo match," Eli comments.

"The best part of that came later," Malik adds. "When we busted out of town on their own cone truck."

"The best part comes *now*," Amber amends, "when

we shut them down once and for all. No clones, no Project Osiris."

"*If* we can pull it off," adds Eli in a nervous tone.

I nod, understanding better than any of them just how incomplete our plan is. Sure, we know who we're looking for and who we have to avoid. We know where our boat is, and we know it has more than half a tank of fuel (enough to get us back to Florida). All the important pieces are in place. But then I think of the balcony, where one lady with insomnia nearly made me a grease spot on the grass. If helping myself to a few bathing suits could go so wrong, who can predict what the coming hours might bring?

We can already see light through the doorframe of our hut. Soon we hear sounds of activity around us—resort employees setting up for the day. I crack the door a touch and peer outside to make sure the coast is clear. Then I lead the others into the open.

Wow. Poseidon by day is really something—water features gleaming in the sun, lush greenery, cascades of flowers, sea-foam green buildings. *Sea-foam*—a word I learned off a tube of oil paint in my attic studio in Serenity.

(No time to think about that. Not now.)

An attendant stocking the towel kiosk offers us a friendly laugh. "You kids must be really eager this morning. The pools don't open for another forty minutes."

The resort is definitely coming to life, though. People are having breakfast on patios and balconies, and young families are out walking with little kids. We're obviously in the open, exposed, but in a way, we're not, because we look like everybody else. We stroll around, smelling bacon, eggs, and toast, and feeling hungry. Malik helps himself to a banana from a display.

As the time ticks down to nine a.m., the walkways bustle, mostly with kids. I scan the passing parade, hoping for a familiar face, but also alert for a different kind of familiar face—an Osiris scientist, or (even worse) a Purple. I see neither. I'm starting to get a sense of how hard it's going to be to track down our six kids in a resort this big and crowded.

A bell sounds, and Poseidon is open for business. The splashing starts immediately, laughter and excited screams drowning out everything else. There's a real traffic jam as kids and some adults carry bulky inner tubes to line up for waterslides. Happy bathers sail by on the lazy river.

"Now what?" asks Eli.

"I guess we go swimming," I reply.

Malik glares at me. "We don't have time for that. We have to track down six people before someone from Poseidon stumbles on our boat."

"Or worse," adds Amber, "one of the Purples stumbles on *us*."

"Look," I say, "we can't very well line up everybody at Poseidon and peer into faces until we find the other six clones. They're going on stuff; we have to go on stuff too."

"Not very scientific," Eli disapproves.

"It kind of is," I argue. "If we circulate, we give ourselves the best chance of seeing the most people."

That's when we discover something unexpected: big, tough Malik is afraid of waterslides.

"Are you serious?" Amber explodes. "You were a beast when you played water polo. The rest of us were scared to get in the pool with you."

"The pool wasn't at the top of a ninety-foot volcano," he says, tight-lipped.

"This isn't a real volcano," Amber reminds him.

"It's still *high*," Malik whines.

I shake my head in amazement. "All the things we've been through, all the times we've almost gotten killed—the least you can do is suck it up for a waterslide that five-year-olds ride every day!"

So we grab inner tubes and join the procession up the stairs to the top of the towering volcano. With our eyes on him, Malik can't weasel out. He doesn't scream, but his face is full of apprehension, his mouth wide open, so he looks like a screamer on mute.

The rest of us follow, twisting and turning down the "lava flow." It's a steep drop and a wild ride (probably a lot of fun if we weren't so stressed). I keep my hands on my hat so it won't fly off.

We hit the bottom of the volcano and shoot off into a huge pool with riders from the other slides. I locate Malik, and if anything, he looks even more agitated than before. He's slumped into the center of his tube and seems to be hiding inside of it.

Amber swims over to him. "Don't be such a baby—"

He grabs her and turns her in the direction he's staring. Her eyes widen.

I follow their gaze to a sturdily built boy about our age. I almost don't recognize him at first because his full head of curly hair is wet and plastered to his scalp.

He has a narrow, angular face and intense eyes I once saw on an internet photograph of the master counterfeiter he's cloned from.

It's Robbie Miers.

22

MALIK BRUDER

Miers!

Considering we've crossed a whole continent looking for him and five others like him, I've never been so
shocked to see anybody in my life. He's our first connection to Project Osiris since we busted out of Happy Valley
that night. Maybe that's why I'm freaking out—this is a big
moment.

Laska is the one with guts enough to approach him.
"Robbie." Her voice is huskier than usual.

He looks at her blankly. I blink. Doesn't he recognize
her? He saw her every day for thirteen years. I think of
my so-called father and his fancy pills designed to make
us kids forget things Osiris doesn't want us to remember.

Have Robbie and the others been medicated so we're wiped from their memories?

And then his eyes are on me. *"Malik?"* All at once, his face is wreathed in smiles. "You're okay! And Tori! Eli!" He turns back to Laska. "Amber? Is that you? You look so different!"

"I cut my hair," she replies. "And dyed it black."

"Was that part of the treatment?" Robbie asks.

"Treatment?" Eli echoes.

"For the sickness," he explains, like that's supposed to mean something to us. "It must have been really bad if you had to go all the way to the hospital in Santa Fe."

We exchange meaningful glances. So that's how Hammerstrom and the other parents have been explaining our absence. We didn't escape. How could anyone be crazy enough to leave America's ideal community? No, we contracted some plague halfway through the Serenity Day fireworks and had to be hauled off to the hospital to keep everybody else from catching it too.

It's a classic Osiris move. If they catch us, they can say we got better. If they don't—well, I guess there's only so much the miracle of modern medicine can do.

Robbie is ecstatic. "This is awesome! We knew Hector

253

was cured. But when you guys didn't come back, we got really worried. It had to be serious if Dr. Bruder couldn't help you!"

We've been out of Happy Valley for weeks, but thirty seconds with Robbie brings it all back to me—the perfect town where nobody learns anything bad. The honesty, harmony, and contentment. Suddenly, I realize that getting ourselves to Poseidon was the *easy* part of this operation. How are we ever going to convince these brainwashed kids that we've come to rescue them? They have no idea that they're clones. They probably don't even know what a clone is. We didn't either until we stumbled on the real internet and looked up Project Osiris. And you can bet they've never heard that name before.

"Listen, Robbie," Eli says grimly. "There's something you have to hear—"

"Not now!" Robbie exclaims. "We've got to find the others! Everybody's going to go nuts when they see you. And just in time for the vacation too!"

I cut him off. "Yeah, yeah, we'll see everybody. But we have to talk to you first."

I look around. We're in a huge pool at the base of seven slides. Fountains and spouts are gushing around us. Every few seconds, new riders splash down, squealing all the way.

The water churns like a storm at sea. The roar of voices is nonstop. It has to be just about the worst place on earth to learn a horrible secret about yourself. But if we go anywhere else, we run the risk of Robbie spotting someone from Happy Valley and calling them over to share the good news that we didn't die of "the sickness."

Right there, in the midst of the sloshing, spraying chaos, Frieden, Laska, Torific, and I circle around Robbie and give him the terrible story: his whole life is an experiment, his parents are scientists, and he's an exact genetic copy of one of the worst human beings ever. We share the telling, taking turns to fill in the gruesome details. This story is too huge to come from any single person.

His first reaction is laughter. He thinks we're joking! Then, slowly, his smirk disappears and his eyes widen. "No!" he cries, shoving me back and breaking away from us. I tackle him and hold him underwater for a few seconds. He's yelling at me, his angry words bubbling to the surface. Luckily, there's so much horseplay going on that nobody notices.

I pull him, choking and gasping, out of the drink. "You have to listen, Robbie! Why would we make this up? You think *we're* happy about it?"

"You're *lying*!" Robbie flails and screams and struggles

as the others start talking again. I lock my arms around him to keep him from bolting. He pounds his fists against my chest and face. I'm not even mad. Just watching Robbie go through in the space of a minute what the four of us had weeks to get used to makes me want to weep for the guy. And trust me, Gus Alabaster's DNA doesn't weep. Never before have I felt such sympathy for anybody.

By this time, Robbie's red face is a mask of pure horror. "You're crazy!" he manages. "Getting sick made you crazy!"

Frieden is amazingly calm and patient. "We've been inside the plastics factory, Robbie. We saw Osiris headquarters with our own eyes."

"Listen to yourselves!" Robbie rants. "Look what the outside world did to you! Breaking rules! Sneaking! Lying! That's not how we were raised!"

"The way we were raised is the biggest lie of all," I insist. "And the second biggest is the people who passed themselves off as our parents!"

"I loved Serenity," Laska adds in a quieter tone. "I believed in our way of life more than anybody. The outside world is messier and meaner and more unfair. But at least it's real."

Robbie shakes free of us and backs away. "The sickness did this to you. I'll get Dr. Bruder. He can help you."

Sudden panic grips me, and it isn't just the prospect of a reunion with my Serenity dad. Sure, we're strong enough to hold Robbie down physically. But then what? Mug him and drag him bodily to the *Gemini*? And five others too? We could never pull that off. We have to convince him—*all* of them.

What if it can't be done? When the four of us accepted the truth about ourselves, we'd seen the proof in the factory and on the internet. And now we expect Robbie and the others to chuck their entire lives and run away on the spur of the moment based on no evidence except our say-so? What were we thinking?

And then a voice behind us says, "Listen to them, Robbie. They're telling the truth."

I wheel. There he is, the waist-deep pool water making his bony legs look even bonier.

Hector.

My fist comes up all by itself. Or maybe it's an Alabaster instinct—I don't think Gus was very forgiving toward the people who sold him out.

Tori grabs my wrist with both hands and hangs on tight. "Stop it!"

"I told you if you ever see me again, you'd better be running!" I shout at Hector.

"Don't hit me!" Hector hisses urgently. "I can help you."

"Like you helped us in Texas?" I demand.

"I can convince them," he promises. "I can get them to believe you. You have to trust me."

I lunge for him again, and this time, my three partners grab me. I don't back off until I catch a glimpse of Robbie, gawking at us. This kind of violent scuffle is something a kid straight out of Happy Valley has never seen before.

But his expression has gone from angry to confused. So Hector's words must mean something to him.

"What's in it for you?" I growl at Hector.

"Wherever you're going, take me with you," he replies.

"In your dreams!"

But Frieden speaks to Hector directly. "We have a boat. If you help us persuade the others to leave with us, we'll take you too."

"No way," I protest. "Nobody gets a second chance to double-cross me!"

"I thought you guys deserted me," Hector whines. "What could I do besides cut a deal?"

"Because you're a slimeball!"

"We're *all* slimeballs," he shoots back. "If you consider

what we're made of, what choice do we have?"

"We have a choice," Frieden states firmly. "If there's one thing we've learned it's that there's always a choice, no matter who you're cloned from."

Robbie is taking this in, his mouth open in wonder. It's as if he still doesn't believe us, but we're so worked up that it can't be just an act for his benefit.

"Robbie," Hector explains. "I was in the Plastics Works with them. I saw what they saw. And I made a deal with the Purples not to tell the rest of you. Nobody was sick—they escaped. And now they're here to save the rest of us."

Robbie is torn in two, like a sheet of paper ripped down the middle. "I should talk to my parents."

"You don't have parents," Amber tells him. "Just scientists in charge of your part of the experiment."

"No," he barely whispers.

"It broke my heart to learn it too," Tori says kindly. "But it's a fact. They raised you. They might even love you. But they're *not* your parents."

For some reason, I remember my fake mother's pot roast. The idea that she's on this island somewhere—and that I can't go see her—puts a lump in my throat the size of a beach ball. After everything I've been through, I'm the same pathetic mama's boy as Robbie. Just a little more used to it, and resigned to my fate.

Robbie's tanned shoulders slump. "Can't I even say good-bye?"

That's when we know we have him.

23

HECTOR AMANI

Okay, I'm not the nicest person in the world. I betrayed my friends in Texas. I don't deny it. What do you expect, considering who I'm cloned from? C. J. Rackoff is a notorious swindler and a complete jerk, but he's also a survivor. Well, me too. Everything I've done has been just trying to survive.

All my life, I've been on the outside looking in. In a town with only thirty kids in total—that wasn't even a real town—I was the fifth wheel nobody wanted. I had to beg Malik and the others to let me escape with them. And when we got separated in the breakout, they just went on without me.

I would have had zero chance on my own. Who could blame me for making my best deal with the only people I'd ever known? And double-crossing my friends? It was the only bargaining chip I had. C. J. Rackoff would have done the same thing. He told me so.

Harsh? You bet. But it's not like those four are cloned from anybody better.

It hurts the most that Malik hates me, since we used to be best friends. Still, when I think back, that was kind of a one-way street too. He kept me around so he could push me around, or so I could help him with his homework. It felt like more at the time, but it wasn't.

Rackoff never would have fallen for it. That's one difference between us.

"I don't trust the shrimp," I overhear Malik whispering to Eli as we dry off at the towel cart. "Not after Texas."

"I'm standing right here," I remind him sharply. "You know my big ears you always made fun of? Well, they can hear you."

Malik rounds on me, face flushed. "Excuse me for not being in love with the guy who stabbed us in the back. I'm not thrilled about giving you another chance to twist the knife."

Amber jumps in. "Cut it out, Malik. This place is crawling with Osiris people—including Purples."

"So he gets a pass for what he did?" Malik demands.

I can't resist. "What choice do you have, Malik? Now that I've seen you here, how do you know I won't rat you out?"

If looks could kill, I'd be dead.

Tori sighs. "If you want us to have faith in you, Hector, you've got to stop saying things like that."

I point at Malik. "He has to stop too."

He glowers at me. "If we can pull this off, we've got a long boat ride at the end. Try anything funny and a lot of sharks will be having indigestion tonight!"

Eli has a question for me. "Where's the best place for us to find the others?"

"I've seen Freddie at the wave pool a lot," I report. "I'm not in the water park as much as everybody else because Rackoff has been trying to play dad lately. He's teaching me how to cheat at blackjack."

Robbie speaks up. "Margaret and Penelope love the lazy river, but one of the moms usually goes with them."

"We definitely want to avoid being seen by any parents," Tori puts in. "And the Purples—forget it. They're the biggest danger of all."

We try the wave pool first. We spread out as we cross the brick walkways. Eli, Malik, and Tori pull their hats low and Amber keeps a hand over her brow. Tori is about six feet to my left when a pained whimper escapes her, and she ducks behind a bathroom hut. Suddenly, the others have melted away too. Amber is off the path, admiring a flowering shrub. Malik veers into a shop and examines a rack of Hawaiian shirts. Eli steps into an outdoor shower and disappears behind the spray of water.

Heading our way, balancing two iced coffees on a tray, is Mr. Pritel—Tori's father. This is the first time she's seen him since the night we broke out of Serenity. Out of all of us, Tori had the closest thing to a real family. I experience a rush of resentment—mostly jealousy. To my own parents, I was only valuable as a lab specimen.

"Hi, Mr. Pritel," I call, and beside me, Robbie waves.

"Morning, Hector. Robbie."

I catch a threatening look from Malik from between the shirts, and I realize he's fully expecting me to give them away. For an instant, I'm tempted to do it, just to pay him back for not trusting me. I can actually feel the words forming on the tip of my tongue.

Mr. Pritel hurries past, and the coast is clear again. As Robbie and I keep walking, the others converge around us, and the mission is back on. Nobody says anything about the close call, least of all Tori. But an expression of grim determination is frozen on her face.

The wave pool is dead ahead. As we get closer, we spy Ben Stastny in the deepest part, jumping breakers.

"Jackpot," I whisper.

Right beside him, bobbing in an inner tube, is Freddie Cinta.

"Ben *and* Freddie!" Eli breathes.

"Two for the price of one," I confirm. As a clone of C. J. Rackoff, I can't resist a bargain.

We're just about to splash into the water when Tori herds us suddenly into a pool cabana.

Malik is annoyed. "What gives, Torific? Are we doing this or what?"

Her reply is one word, but it speaks volumes: "Purple."

We take turns peering out through the canvas drapery. I remember that about Tori—real eagle eyes. There, in another cabana across the curved rim of the pool, is the Purple People Eater we call Rump L. Stiltskin. He's in Bermuda shorts and a muscle shirt, and he's pretending to read a book. But it's pretty clear he's keeping an eye on Freddie and Ben.

Eli frowns. "I guess we could wait till he goes to the bathroom or something. But that might be hours."

Tori thinks it over. "Well, obviously we can't all go out there." She turns to Robbie and me. "You belong here.

You'll have to do it. Get them out of the pool and meet us at the path down to the lazy river."

"What if Rump follows us?" I ask her.

"He won't."

"How can you be so sure?" I'm a wheeler-dealer. Stuff that happens in the real physical world isn't my strength.

Tori blinks. "You let us worry about that."

Robbie doesn't say much as we splash out into the pool. He looks stunned—which is the way I must have looked when I first realized the truth.

"Don't overthink it," I advise him. "Not unless you want your head to explode."

"You look nothing like him," he blurts.

"Huh?"

"Mr. Rackoff. If you have his DNA, how come you don't look alike?"

"We will—when I'm as old as he is now." Not a fun thing to admit. But if I'm stuck with his face, maybe I'll be rich like him too. "And you're going to look like some counterfeiter. And Freddie and Ben—you get the picture."

He shakes his head in wonder. "I still can't believe it. I mean, I believe you guys. I just don't believe—you know—*it*."

"At least you already know," I tell him. "Poor Freddie

and Ben still have their happy surprise coming up."

We're up to our shoulders and jumping waves by the time we reach them.

"Hi, Robbie," Ben calls.

Notice there's no *Hi, Hector* in there. Rackoff may be loaded, but I'll bet he was never very popular either. Anyway, I'm used to it. Accidentally or on purpose, Freddie splashes me in the face.

I've got one eye on Rump L. Stiltskin in his cabana. He's definitely watching us, but there's no reason for him to be suspicious.

All right, Tori. Whatever you're going to do, do it now!

As if on cue, Rump's cabana collapses on him, and he's tangled in metal poles and canvas drapery. As his arms and legs struggle against the smothering fabric, I spy Tori and Eli scampering through the maze of deck chairs away from the scene of the crime.

"All, right, you guys," I bark. "Come with us. Now!"

"Why?" asks Ben.

"It's really important," Robbie chimes in. "Let's go!"

We struggle through the breakers, Ben pulling Freddie in the inner tube. When we climb up on the deck, I can see that the undulating arms and legs in the wreckage of Rump's cabana are close to escape.

"Run," I order.

Maybe it's the urgency in my voice; maybe it's the fact that Robbie runs first. Or maybe criminal DNA is always good at crunch time. We take off, heading past the entrance to the lazy river into the cover of the trees.

Once we're out of view of the wave pool, we pull up, catching our breath.

"What's this about?" Freddie wheezes.

Eli steps into the clearing. "We've got something to tell you."

"Eli?" Ben is wide-eyed. He's even more shocked when Tori, Amber, and Malik join the group.

"You're cured!" Freddie exclaims in delight.

"We were never sick," Malik informs him. "Now, listen up. And get ready to have your minds blown."

24

AMBER LASKA

Freddie doesn't believe us. I can tell by the way his lower lip sticks out. Or maybe he does believe us, but he doesn't *want* to.

It's way more than accepting a new set of facts. It's giving up your whole life, and everything you ever knew and loved. I did it because I saw hard evidence. Robbie and Freddie and Ben have to take the leap just because we say so.

"I knew there had to be something messed up about Serenity," Ben muses.

Freddie is stubborn. "No way."

"It wasn't so much when we were *there*," Robbie puts in. "Then we didn't have anything to compare it to. But now that we're out, meeting people—a lot of the things our folks told us just don't add up."

"A vacation resort isn't the same as the real world," Freddie points out.

Listening to them brings back the days when the others knew the truth about Serenity, but I was too programmed to see it. I was as blind as Freddie. Even more so, because my mother was our teacher, so she had extra time to drum the un-facts into my head.

Ben looks torn. "I don't know. Have you turned on the TV here? The shows aren't the same as what we got in Serenity."

Freddie's appalled. "You watched TV? After our parents told us not to?"

"That's something you learn about the real world," Malik puts in. "People don't always do what they're told. They lie sometimes. It's actually pretty awesome—"

I silence him with an elbow to the ribs. "You're not helping." Leave it to Malik to make a speech when the clock is ticking.

"Project Osiris is the lie," Eli insists. "They told you we were in the hospital—another lie. Here we are, not sick. And the last time we were in Serenity, it was a ghost town."

I'm in agony over the very real possibility that we won't be able to convince them. Nothing could be worse than that powerlessness. "You're not on vacation," I plead. "Project

Osiris is *hiding* here. When we escaped, they had to leave the country, because we could put them in jail with what we know."

They have a million questions—they *should* have a million questions considering what we're asking them to do. But we haven't got time to answer them. The longer we spend on West Cay, the greater the chance that we'll be spotted by someone from Serenity. And that's not the only time pressure we're under. Rump L. Stiltskin is probably already looking for Freddie and Ben, and Hector and Robbie have been unaccounted for even longer than they have. Sure, people get separated in a place like this. But sooner or later, Osiris is going to realize that the disappearance of their clones is more than a coincidence. When that happens, we need to be *gone.*

"When we get to the boat," Tori promises, "we'll show you the web page on Project Osiris. We can prove all of this. Just not now."

"They can," Hector confirms. "I've seen it."

"So bust a move," Malik orders.

And they follow us, even Freddie. Somehow, being pushed around by Malik is an old, familiar feeling that calms everybody's nerves in a crisis. It's about time his obnoxious personality came in handy.

Next stop: the lazy river. We stake out the river-bank along the artificial waterway, hoping Margaret and Penelope will float by soon. Actually, we hope they float by at all. Our luck, we've chosen the one morning when the girls decide to ride the slides or go to the beach first thing.

Eli, Malik, Tori, and I hide in the bushes, leaving Hector, Robbie, Freddie, and Ben standing by the water's edge. It feels like a hundred years, but in reality, it's more like eight or ten minutes. At one point, we see Rump L. Stiltskin crossing the footbridge over the rapids. He never glances down, though, to see the object of his search.

There are a lot of people on the lazy river, at least half of them adults, so I almost miss Mrs. Rauha as she passes. Another Serenity adult, coplotter of the Osiris deception. She's got her back turned as Margaret and Penelope come bobbing along. Convenient.

The girls spot the boys and call out greetings.

"You have to come with us!" Hector hisses.

"We'll catch you guys later," Penelope calls back.

"Get them out, shrimp!" Malik hollers beside me.

Hector stretches and grabs Margaret's arm, but the momentum of the tube yanks him off his feet and he tumbles into the lazy river. The four of us abandon the bushes and rush down to the water, where Robbie, Freddie, and

Ben are rescuing Hector instead of hauling out the girls.

Penelope and Margaret are laughing, but that stops when they get a look at us.

"Eli?" Penelope cries in amazement.

In a Herculean effort, Malik lifts both girls clean out of their tubes and is about to topple into the water himself when Tori grabs him around the midsection. There we teeter, fighting gravity, as Mrs. Rauha's tube bumps the side and turns her around to see what's going on with her girls. Her eyes widen first in shock and then in horror as she identifies the four Osiris escapees.

She begins to struggle, attempting to paddle back against the current toward us. But she's already thirty feet downstream. As a single figure we keel over onto the bank and break apart into individuals.

"*Stop!*" Mrs. Rauha shrieks, and swings around the corner out of sight.

"Mom—?" Margaret begins.

"No time to explain!" Eli cuts her off. "Come with us. It's an emergency."

The girls look at us uncertainly. The fact that we're here and not dying in a hospital in Santa Fe doesn't explain anything, but it seems to communicate that the situation is as urgent as we say it is. And the fact that other Serenity kids are with us persuades them even more.

We scramble up the grassy bank to the pathway. There are ten of us now—all the Osiris clones except one.

"What about Aldwin?" I pant.

"We can't save him," Tori replies sadly.

"We came for *everybody*!" I challenge my best friend. "There are eleven of us, not ten!"

She's unmoved. "If we don't get to the boat right now, we'll be caught. Mrs. Rauha saw us. As soon as she can get to a phone, she'll sound the alarm."

"What are you *saying*?" My outrage is swelling. "Aldwin didn't happen to be in the right place to get rescued, so tough luck, he doesn't get a life? How's that fair?"

I feel a gentle hand on my arm. Malik. "We got ten, Laska. We did amazing."

"Ten's not eleven!"

"If we push it, we'll get zero," he insists.

I want to scream: *That's not right!* The right thing to do is always so clear to me—like it's directly overhead in skywriting. Why can't Malik see that? Why can't Tori?

And yet—

I'm cloned from someone who also thought she was always doing the right thing. And Mickey Seven went on to be one of the most notorious terrorists in history.

For once in my life, I have to abandon my instincts and follow the others.

Margaret is bewildered. "Why are you talking about my mother like she's the enemy?"

"You'll have to trust us," Eli says briskly. "We'll explain later."

"No!" Penelope exclaims. "I'm not moving until you tell me what's going on!"

"Then you can be caught too!" Malik snaps. "Give my regards to Aldwin!"

It's a good thing Margaret and Penelope grew up with Malik. Otherwise, they'd be running in the opposite direction.

"Spread out!" Tori orders in an undertone. Even in a busy water park, a stampede of ten kids would attract attention we can't afford.

We separate into clusters of two and three, jogging rather than sprinting, following Tori and Eli in the lead. I hear the others breathing hard around me, and the dull rhythm of their bare feet on the pathways. Short, slight, unathletic Hector is especially struggling, soaking wet from head to toe, the fabric of his bathing suit swishing with every stride. Thanks to my workout routine, I'm feeling strong.

I keep a close eye on Margaret and Penelope, who can't possibly trust us. At least the boys have enough information to make up their minds whether or not to believe our story. The girls are with us on blind faith alone. At the same time, I scan left and right, hoping to catch a glimpse of Aldwin. Maybe we can't search the entire resort for him. But if we happen to run into him, nobody could argue that he shouldn't come along.

The crowd thins out as we approach the edge of the water park. From there, it's just a quarter-mile to where we left the boat. I'm beginning to think that we might actually pull this off when I spot her.

Mom.

God help me, for a split second I'm thrilled to see her. Unbelievable! In spite of everything, part of me actually *misses* the bogus mother who deceived me every day of my life. Who pretended to love me while studying me for signs that I might be turning into the terrorist I was cloned from. How *weak* I am!

But before I can wrap my mind around those whirling thoughts, a new emotion takes over: raw fear. How can we get caught when we're *so* close? And by *her*, of all people?

I wait for the startled recognition, the accusing finger pointed in my direction. It doesn't happen.

Doesn't she see me?

She's wearing earbuds, lost in the world of her music. I angle my face away from her, watching out of the corner of my eye.

She casts a friendly wave in the direction of Margaret and Penelope, yet somehow manages to miss her own "daughter." I pass an uneasy few seconds, worrying that the girls might give us away. They have no reason to go along with us. But they smile and wave back, if a little uneasily. They've got more guts than we give them credit for. After all, they're cloned from criminals too.

And then a voice over my opposite shoulder exclaims, "Mrs. Laska, help! They're trying to take us away!"

Freddie breaks from Malik and Ben and rushes toward my Serenity mother.

That gets her attention and then some. She tears off her sunglasses, sending them flying. Aghast, she stares from face to face until her gaze falls on me. Her oh-so-familiar eyes burn through me like lasers. Her shriek is unearthly.

"Amber!!"

She reaches into the pocket of her shorts and pulls out her phone. I make a bull run at her, throwing myself at her knees. The impact knocks her over backward. Tori rips the phone from her hand and hurls it into a kiddie pool.

We're both rolling in the dirt when she says, "Amber—sweetheart —"

I'm astounded. "You're delusional! Do you honestly think I'll fall for that? Are you so crazy that you think we can go back to the way things used to be?"

Malik hauls me to my feet and shoves me in the direction of our boat.

Freddie grabs Ben by the arm, spinning him around. "Don't go!" he begs.

But after a moment's hesitation, Ben shakes him off and joins our getaway, running down the path. The girls look really scared, but they stick with us too. We leave the water park and turn on the jets, making for the line of palm trees that marks the edge of West Cay. Beyond that, we know, is the sandbar where we beached the *Gemini*. Escape is that close. I feel bad about Aldwin, and even a little bit about Freddie. But nine clones living in freedom is better than eleven under the jackboot of Project Osiris.

We burst out of the trees and stand on the beach, staring at our boat—or at least what we can see of it. Only the wheelhouse and the light at the top of the mast are above water.

Malik gawks at the *Gemini*'s bridge, tilted at an odd angle and rocking with the gentle waves. "Where's the rest of it?"

I'm too devastated to point out what a truly idiotic question that is. "It sank!"

"How?" Malik demands.

Eli's face is ashen. "We must have put a hole in the bottom when we ran it aground on that sandbar," he moans. "All day long, while we've been running around saving people, our only way out has been *sinking*!"

His despair bubbles into me in the form of pure anger and frustration. The Mickey Seven in me wants to break something—or maybe it isn't her at all, and I'm just plain rotten. Anyway, the only thing around to break is the boat, and it's already broken.

The shocked silence is shattered by a staccato peal of laughter. Hector has sat down in the sand and is cackling at the sight of the sunken wreck as if nothing has ever been funnier.

Malik hauls him up by one skinny arm. "*You* did this!"

"How could I?" Hector defends himself. "Nobody told me where the boat was."

"You ratted us out to Osiris! They found the boat and sank it!"

"I've been with you the whole time!" Hector protests. "Every single minute!"

"Then why are you laughing?" I snarl.

"Because when you're me, you expect everything to go wrong. If you don't laugh, you cry."

"Leave him alone, Malik," I grumble. "It's not his fault we're in this mess."

Malik drops Hector back to the beach.

Penelope speaks up. "I don't get it. Where were we supposed to go in that boat?"

"Away from *here*," Eli replies bitterly. "Away from our parents, who aren't really—never mind. It's all over now."

"Not necessarily." Tori steps forward. "There's a whole marina on the other side of the hotel. They've got a lot of boats. We stole this one; we can steal another."

"Steal?" Robbie echoes in amazement.

He's goggling at us, and so are the others. I look at them and see myself—innocent, clueless, brainwashed Serenity kids. They're fresh out of the land of honesty, harmony, and contentment. People don't even tell lies there, much less break the law. To Robbie, Ben, Margaret, and Penelope, we might as well have just said we're going to levitate off the beach and fly out of here.

In spite of our dire situation, I can't help smiling. "It's time to grab your criminal DNA and take it out for a test-drive."

25

ELI FRIEDEN

No way can we cut through the water park now. Mrs. Laska and Mrs. Rauha must be already sounding the alarm, and we can't forget Rump L. Stiltskin. It's been more than half an hour since Ben and Freddie vanished from his view in the wave pool, and he's got to be anxious. Who knows how many Purples he's got out there searching for them?

Our strategy is to hike along the coastline. That way, we can get to the marina while avoiding the crowded Poseidon attractions where Project Osiris will be looking for us. It's certainly not the most direct path. Just around the bend from the sunken *Gemini*, the beach ends, to be replaced by an outcropping of rocky coral.

"Can we climb it?" I suggest.

"If you're a mountain goat," grumbles Malik, peering

up at the jagged, inhospitable rocks without much enthusiasm.

"We could make it," Tori muses, "but it's probably better to cut inland around it. We'd be too easy to spot going over the top. Plus it's rough terrain to cover barefoot."

The inland route has its own problems, though. The trees are thick and slow us down. I can't shake the image of parents and Purples converging from all over the resort, sharing what they know, and making plans to capture us. Our one advantage was the element of surprise—they weren't expecting us. Now that's gone, and every wasted minute gives them more time to get organized and come after us.

We slog along over rough terrain, finally breaking through to another sandy cove. Then we're back in the trees, stumbling over rocks, struggling to keep the ocean in sight. Sobbing is the soundtrack to our journey. Amber is bringing Margaret and Penelope up to speed on what they are and mostly what they *aren't*. Considering that story is old news to me by now, it's amazing how much it hurts every time I hear it.

Soon the trees thin out, and we're approaching another cove. We know instantly there's something different about this one. A cacophony of sound reaches us—laughter, excitement, screams. For an instant I'm afraid we've made a wrong turn and we're back at the water park. No, but it's almost as bad. It's the resort's main beach, and it's crawling with people.

I stop dead and everybody rear-ends me.

Tori reads my mind. "They're looking for us in the water park, not the beach. We can lose ourselves in the big crowd."

And it works. We thread our way through towels and umbrellas, dodging Frisbees and avoiding volleyball games. My eyes scan the sunbathers, searching for familiar faces and hoping not to find them. Every single step I'm expecting to be tackled from the rear by an unseen Purple People Eater. It's a long walk that feels a lot longer, but at last the trees beckon from the other side of the beach.

Behind me, I hear Hector breathe, "We made it."

That's when I see him—a tall, lean Asian boy who used to live three doors down from me. He's sitting on a beach blanket, surrounded by more shells than one ocean could possibly offer, and he's got them all organized by size, by shape, by color, in endless rows and patterns.

Aldwin Wo, the last of the Osiris clones.

Malik notices me noticing. "Keep walking," he intones.

I stop in my tracks. "We can't leave him here. Not when

we have a chance to save him."

"I'm with Malik," Hector puts in. "When he recognizes you guys, he could make a scene in front of the whole beach."

Even Tori seems unsure. "It could be risky, Eli."

Amber doesn't say a word. She's already marching across the sand toward Aldwin.

It takes Aldwin a few seconds to recognize her. But when he does, he's up on his feet, hugging her. Suddenly, all the color drains from him, so we know Amber's telling him the hard truth.

Our eyes are on them, which is why we don't see who's coming up behind us.

"Hi, kids. Long time no see." The voice is oily, full of false friendliness.

We wheel. Sunburned bald head. Bony elbows and knees sticking out of a Hawaiian shirt and shorts. Bad posture that reminds us of Hector's—and for very good reason.

It's C. J. Rackoff, grinning into our shocked faces. "I believe the phrase you're looking for is 'The jig is up.'"

Malik is the first of us to find his voice. "Some mastermind *you* are!" he snorts. "Count much? There are ten of us and only one of you!"

That's when we see two large figures striding across the sand toward us. It's General Confusion and Screaming Mimi, their grim expressions carved from stone. You never get anger from Purple People Eaters, just cold efficiency.

"You're still outnumbered!" Hector sputters a lot less certainly.

"Am I?" Rackoff asks mildly. "Poor me."

Even defiant Malik understands his meaning. Purples are trained commandos. And let's face it, we're just a bunch of kids. All we can do is watch helplessly as the two paramilitary men close in on us.

And then the metal pole of a large beach umbrella swings out of nowhere, catching the two Purples full in the face. Both men drop to the beach, unconscious. Amber stands over them, jaw stuck out, an avenging angel in a bathing suit.

Malik takes advantage of the distraction to ram his head full force into Rackoff's jaw. The former embezzler goes down, dazed.

"*That's* for ruining Hector's life!" Malik rasps.

"I *gave* him his life," Rackoff manages through swollen and bleeding lips. "He wouldn't exist if not for me."

Malik's reply is barely a snarl. "That's another thing for you to pay for!"

We're not blending in with the vacationers anymore. Half the beach is staring at us in horrified amazement. There are hundreds of kids at Poseidon, but only the clones of criminal masterminds could take out three grown men in the space of a few seconds.

Screaming Mimi stirs and sits up with a groan. Amber shoves him down again with the umbrella pole.

Tori begins herding us up the beach. "Let's get out of here!"

One advantage of not being anonymous anymore—people get out of your way. Towels are pulled aside; Frisbee-ers and volleyball players leap clear as we exit the beach, accelerating to a run. There are ten of us now—Aldwin is bringing up the rear, keeping pace with Amber, who has dropped her weapon in the interest of speed. He's looking at her with a mixture of respect and fear. And—yikes—behind them I see Rackoff and General Confusion staggering along in pursuit. The General is barking into his phone.

"In a couple of minutes we're going to have all of Osiris on our necks!" I call to Tori, my words coming out in gasps.

"The marina!" she exclaims, pointing toward Poseidon's palace—the central hotel and casino. Beyond it lies

West Cay's main harbor. But the entire water park stands in our way.

For the first time, I can pick out the Serenity presence in the bustling resort. They're the ones pushing purposefully through the vacationers. Faces bubble out of the throng, heading in our direction—Purple People Eaters and Osiris parents. I see Mrs. Amani, Mr. Cinta, Dr. Bruder. There she is again—Mrs. Laska, Mr. Pritel at her side.

There are more—just about every adult we grew up with. But there's no point in recognizing people in the crowd. The marina is too far away, and our enemies are too close. We're not going to make it.

"Over here!" Tori scrambles down the bank of the lazy river and begins yanking on the rubber side of a motorized maintenance raft.

Seizing on that faint hope, we join her, and haul the light craft down the grassy slope and drag it into the water.

"Get in!" Tori orders, yanking the cord to start the outboard motor.

We attract a lot of attention on the lazy river—ten kids piling onto a raft built for five. At first, a traffic jam of inner tubes backs up behind us, people craning their necks to see what the holdup is. Our pursuers race down the bank, arms out to grab us.

"Hit the gas!" Malik howls.

The little engine engages and we shoot off down the lazy river, bumping tubes out of our way, apologizing as we overturn a few, dumping people into the water. Purples sprint along the side, trying to keep up with us, even as we slalom around the bobbing resort guests.

"Faster, Tori! Faster!" I exhort.

"It won't go any faster!" she calls back. "We've got too much weight on it!"

In spite of that, we're putting some distance between us and our pursuers.

We pass a wide-eyed Poseidon attendant. "Hey, you kids can't—"

We never get to hear what we can't, but it's a good guess it has something to do with driving an overloaded maintenance raft at top speed on a lazy river full of people.

We flash past him and round the corner, nearly sending Hector rolling over the inflatable side. At the last second, Malik reaches out, grabs a flailing ankle, and hauls his former best friend aboard.

"Thanks!" Hector quavers.

"I thought you were somebody else!" Malik growls back.

I peer up the grassy bank and see the hotel towers

looming directly above us. The next bend will leave us moving in the wrong direction as the lazy river curves back toward the water park. We'll never get closer than we are right now.

"Hit the brakes!" I bawl at Tori.

Tori understands instantly. Without slowing down, she steers us onto the bank. The small craft hurtles up the slope and flips, dumping us all onto the grass. For an instant, everything goes dark as a lot of bodies and a rubber raft fall on top of me.

With a roar of exertion, Malik hurls the boat away, and we leap to our feet just in time to see an army of Osiris pursuers bearing down on us from the direction of the water park.

"The hotel!" I cry, racing for the heavy doors.

On the other side of the building lies the marina and escape. We have a head start. But will it be enough time to hot-wire a boat and head out to sea?

We blast through the doors into the plush lobby with its soaring ceiling and walls of fish tanks. I look around desperately. There's the casino, the elevators, the restaurant—my gaze follows a long corridor with daylight at the end. That has to be it—the exit to the marina.

"This way!"

I'm in the lead, so I see him first, blocking my way, flanked by two Purple People Eaters. My heart begins to pound hard against the inside of my rib cage. An arctic chill comes over me.

He's wearing a sport jacket and no tie, his only concession to the casual resort surroundings. Yet there's nothing casual about the fury in his expression.

Felix Frieden—Hammerstrom.

My father.

We keep running. I don't know if we can take them, but we have to try. Any chance to make a life for ourselves has come down to this time and this place. To lose now is to lose everything.

My one-time father reaches into the pocket of his blazer, pulls out a shiny black object, and points it at me.

A pistol.

That stops us in our tracks. We're from Serenity, where violence is completely unheard of. We barely even knew there was such a thing as a gun, much less had one aimed at us by our beloved mayor and school principal.

The lobby is mostly deserted this time of day, but the few hotel guests who are around fearfully scoop up their children and flee. Hammerstrom turns to the cowed staff behind the reception desk and gestures toward the exit with the pistol. "Leave, please."

Grateful to be off the hook, they hurry outside. The pistol swings back to me, and I raise my arms in surrender, paralyzed by fear. It's not the first time my life has been in danger, but it's the first time the threat comes from a weapon specifically designed to kill, wielded by someone ruthless enough to use it.

My gesture seems to irritate him. "Why would you even know to do that? It isn't something Mrs. Laska taught in Contentment class. Don't you see the *contamination* you've brought down on us?"

"*I'm* the contamination?" I can hardly believe the irony. "Where's the part in our perfect life where your own father threatens to shoot you?"

The sound of running feet on the stone floor behind us makes us all wheel. It's our pursuers from the water park catching up at last. They pull up short at the sight of us there, held at gunpoint in our bathing suits, dripping water on the granite.

If there was a way out before, it's gone now. We're outnumbered and surrounded. The other kids are petrified, but for Malik, Amber, Tori, and me, it's different. We're scared, sure, and devastated that we couldn't rescue our fellow clones. Still, this is a moment we've always known might come. Since escaping Serenity, we've made it farther than any of us could have imagined. Yet our amazing run has reached its end.

Hammerstrom's rage is ice cold. "We gave you every-thing—fine homes, loving parents, a lifestyle unheard of anywhere else. And how do you repay us? By destroying everything."

"There was nothing to destroy," Malik speaks up resent-fully. "It was all fake—even us." He catches a glimpse of his mother in the group behind us and quickly turns away. "Especially us."

Mr. Pritel steps forward and places a gentle hand on Tori's shoulder. "Torific . . ."

She shakes him off and refuses even to look at him.

"You've got some nerve blaming us for ruining every-thing!" Amber seethes. "You gave us lives that were ruined from the start. Human clones—we were a crime before we were even born. Made with the DNA of master criminals. And your so-called research—*that* was the most evil thing of all."

My former father's rage disappears and is replaced by sheer astonishment. "How can you say that? There was never anything more optimistic and positive than Project

Osiris! In you, we took some of the worst of humanity and proved that, given the right circumstances, it could be *good*. Don't you understand what that means? It's like a second chance for the entire human race. The nature-versus-nurture debate is over! In the future, we might not need prisons. The legal system as we know it will be a thing of the past!"

"Except it didn't work," I interrupt.

His face darkens. "It *did* work! It was *working*! It was *you*, Eli! You had to interfere with the course of science!"

For the first time, it occurs to me that Felix Hammerstrom isn't 100 percent evil. What he is, actually, is crazy. I don't know if he started out that way, or if Project Osiris turned him. When you create a totally bogus reality to raise kids in, you have to live in that world too. And eventually, you can't tell the difference between what's real and what isn't.

Believe it or not, it actually makes me hate him a little less, and almost feel sorry for him.

I say a word I never thought I'd speak again. "Dad . . ."

"Silence!" he bellows, pale with fury. His arm rises until the pistol is pointed directly at my chest.

Dr. Bruder speaks up. "Felix—don't!"

"It's not too late to save our work!" Hammerstrom tosses back. "Eli is the ringleader! If you want to kill a snake, cut off its head!"

His pistol arm stiffens.

He's going to shoot me, I think to myself. I should be screaming, begging, fleeing, flattening myself to the floor. Instead, I'm numb with the understanding that part of me expected it to end this way. What do you do with an experiment that fails? Wash it down the sink.

His finger whitens on the trigger.

"No!" A slight, bony figure pushes past me and hurls himself at Hammerstrom. Hector slams into my one-time father from the side, jarring his gun arm. With a sharp crack, the shot goes off.

The display front of the huge tank over the reception desk shatters into a million pieces. Shards of broken glass rain down on us, followed by a deluge of water. It knocks the feet out from under us and sends us sliding across the lobby. Fish and sea creatures drop from above, hit the floor, and flap around in wild distress. I look up just in time to see an immense black shape descending upon us, blotting out the lights.

I push Tori clear, rolling and skidding after her. The giant manta ray, weighing easily a ton or more, comes down with a tremendous thud. I see Hammerstrom disappear under the titanic wingspan just before the mighty splash lifts me up and sends me spinning.

Poseidon is a disorienting blur of water, bodies, and fish, until, at last, the wall swings around to meet me. Everything goes black.

26

MALIK BRUDER

I end up with a snapping turtle standing on my stomach, looking down at me.

I push him off and jump up, slipping and sliding on the wet floor. The lobby is totally nuts. People are lying all over the place, and there's some serious screaming going on. Plus a lot of fish are flopping around us now that the water's drained away. I never paid much attention in science class, but I don't think this can be very good for them. The shark isn't moving. I'm pretty sure he's dead, poor guy.

I pick up a small ray and toss it into the fountain—it's the only water around. That's not going to be an option for his great-granddaddy, the ginormous manta ray that takes up half the lobby floor. That's when I notice a pair of feet sticking out from under it.

Felix Hammerstrom.

To my surprise, I kind of feel bad about it. Sure, he was awful, but what a way to go. Besides, somebody getting killed is nothing to celebrate. Reason number fifty why I'm not as much like Gus as I thought.

"Malik," comes a voice.

I practically jump out of my skin. It's my dad—I mean, Dr. Bruder. I back away fearfully.

"It's all right, Malik," he says gently. "Nobody is going to hurt you."

"I'd feel a lot better hearing that from a Purple," I retort.

"Project Osiris is over," he promises. "You have nothing to fear from us anymore."

"Good."

He hangs around, like there should be more to talk about, but I freeze him out. I should be relieved—and in a way I am. The gnawing terror of being caught and re-brainwashed, and dragged back to that un-life in Happy Valley is gone. Still, it's not enough, not even close. For nearly fourteen years, this person lied to me and pretended to be my *father*! And when I think about my *mother*—

No. I can't go there. It's too much to wrap my mind around at a crazy time like this. "Beat it," I tell him in a voice that's more sad than angry.

I watch him retreat to his fellow mad scientists. They look shocked and scared, which is exactly what they deserve. It's almost as if, while Hammerstrom was alive, they didn't notice what a sick, twisted, illegal experiment they've been part of. And now that he's dead, the truth came crashing down on them the way the giant ray came crashing down on their boss.

Are we expected to cut them slack for that? *Oh, hey, no harm, no foul. We were only following orders . . .*

Sorry, I can't get to that forgiving place. Too much was done to us for too long.

That's when I see Hector, practically lying at my feet. Who would believe it—that backstabbing little worm is a hero! He saved Eli's life, and maybe the rest of us too. I feel so many emotions at the same time—good and bad. It's *so* Hector. He sells us out, and just when I'm getting used to the idea of hating his guts, he has to go and do something like this.

I pick him up and he opens one beady eye. Hammerstrom's bullet must have grazed him, because he's got an angry red line stretching from the corner of his mouth to his left ear.

"You stupid little shrimp!" I rage. "You almost got yourself killed!"

He breaks into a goofy grin. "We're friends again."

"Fat lot of good it would have done if that bullet had gone straight through your empty head instead of along your cheek!"

He reaches a hand to his face. It comes away bloody. "Is it bad?"

"You're still ugly, if that's what you're asking. It didn't make you any better looking." But I spoil the moment by locking him in a bear hug. I've said it before—I'm too nice.

I survey the wreckage of the lobby. People are lifting themselves out of the puddles on the floor amid the dead fish, squirming turtles, and seaweed. Tori and Amber are huddled together, looking stunned, but alive and well. Eli is standing over the hulk of the manta, shaking a little. I can relate. Crushed underneath that humongous fish is what's left of the only father he's ever going to get. The fact that Hammerstrom was worse than slime doesn't change that.

The other Osiris kids are okay too, although they're pretty shaken up. We've been living this horror movie for weeks, but they've had to digest the whole thing in half a morning. All that Serenity baloney swept away in the blink of an eye.

From the ranks of the Osiris researchers, Freddie steps forward timidly. I give him a forgiving nod. How can we blame him for not believing the unbelievable? How can we hold that against him? We clones are a pretty exclusive club, and it's not like a membership drive would make it any bigger. No way can we kick out one of our own.

The heavy doors are flung open and in burst about twenty Poseidon security personnel. They stop dead at the sight of the shattered aquarium tank and the disaster on the lobby floor. At the rear of this army marches a commanding figure, tall with iron-gray hair. She wears an elegant business suit and on her feet are immaculate white sneakers.

Tamara Dunleavy is walking alongside some big shot from Poseidon, and this guy's losing his mind over the state of his hotel. He keeps going on and on about the manta ray and how hard it's going to be to get a new one. I guess that's true. You can't just order them up from MantaRaysRUs .com.

"In case you haven't noticed," Ms. Dunleavy informs him impatiently, "there is a body underneath that ray."

That shuts the doofus up pretty quick.

Then she spies Eli, safe and sound, and in that instant, CEO Tamara is gone, replaced by a frantic, relieved parent. She practically wipes out fifteen times splashing across the fish-strewn lobby to throw her arms around her clone.

"Eli—thank God!"

Frieden hugs her back and nods sadly in the direction of the manta. "It's him. My—Dr. Hammerstrom."

"Poor Felix. He was brilliant, in spite of it all." She steps back and sighs. "How are the others?"

"Everybody's okay," Eli confirms. "All eleven—subjects."

Torific speaks up. "But Ms. Dunleavy—why are you here? You said you couldn't do anything because of what Hammerstrom knew about you."

"That's not going to be a problem," she replies with a wan look in the direction of the ray.

"But that just happened," Laska persists. "You couldn't have known about it when you started out."

"Well, I realized where you were going, of course. I'm not stupid. And I decided I mustn't abandon you, no matter what the cost. I'm responsible for what happens to you. And now I'm the only one who can make it right."

Billionaires can say stuff like that, because they can get away with almost anything, just by throwing money at it. Busted-up lobby? No problem. Dead manta ray? Put it on my tab.

The dead guy *under* the manta ray turns out to be a bit trickier, since the West Cay police have to be involved. But one call to the US Embassy in Nassau and the deputy ambassador is on a plane to come straighten it out for us.

The very best part of this lousy day is the looks on the faces of the former Osiris researchers and Purple People Eaters when the eleven of us waltz out of there to get on Ms. Dunleavy's private jet while they're still stuck in the middle of the investigation. That's sweeter than sugar.

I'm tempted to call something like, "Hey, losers, where's your contentment now?" Because none of them seem very contented. In fact, they look devastated.

But I don't say anything at all. I've got parents in there, and mixed feelings about what's going to happen to them. Not that any punishment could undo what they did to us for all those years.

Revenge may be important in Gus Alabaster's world, but it's not such a big deal to me.

27

ELI FRIEDEN

Amber is making to-do lists again. Not about exercising and a healthy diet and practicing stuff—although she has gone back to playing the harpsichord in Ms. Dunleavy's music room.

I catch a glimpse of her latest:

THINGS TO DO TODAY (UNPRIORITIZED)

- Buy new boat for owner of the *Gemini*
- Reimburse Poseidon guests for stolen swimsuits/hats
- Replace motorcycles (2) taken from Boss Hawg's roadhouse
- Pay for damages to New Hope Soup Kitchen
- Compensate Girl Scouts of America for 94 boxes of cookies . . .

It goes clear back to our escape from Serenity. Amber wants to make sure we pay for all the damage we had to do and the things we had to steal in our long adventure. I think she's trying to prove that she's not Mickey Seven. Or maybe she's just a nice person.

Hey, I support her 100 percent. I felt worse than anybody about breaking into houses and hotel rooms, and taking clothes and food and cars—doing anything and everything just to stay free.

I'm not so sure about the Girl Scout Cookies, though, and I tell Amber so.

She's unmoved. "It's not *what* you stole, it's the fact that you stole it. Tori sold most of those and both you guys ate the rest. This is our chance to make amends."

Come to think of it, that's exactly how you'd expect Mickey Seven to be: unyielding, my way or the highway. It was what got her thrown in jail in the first place—the extremes she went to, anyway. I'd like to believe Amber has a little more common sense. Then again, Amber would starve before she'd eat as many Girl Scout Cookies as we did. The memory of Tori and me, side by side on the concrete floor of that warehouse, inhaling Thin Mints and Rah-Rah Raisins, is going to stay with me always.

I don't think Amber and Malik had moments like that.

Not the way they argue. They even fight over Gus Alabaster's last words, which Malik refuses to reveal because, "It's a private thing between us Alabaster men."

Of course, Amber won't leave it alone. "I know what it was," she needles him. "He said you're inheriting his fortune and you won't admit it because you're too cheap to share."

Or, "He warned you never to get mixed up in a life of crime."

Or, "He didn't tell you anything at all and you're clamming up because having a big secret makes you feel important."

That's the straw that breaks the camel's back. "He did so tell me something!"

"Oh, yeah? Spill it."

Malik fixes her with eyes that are barely slits. "Just this once," he growls, "I'm going to tell you my private business, if you promise to shut up about it from now on. Deal?" He takes a deep breath. "He called me a *giff*."

"A giff?" Tori frowns. "What's a giff?"

Malik shrugs. "Gangsters have these words for stuff—a mook. A babbo. I looked *giff* up on Google, but there's nothing." He's acting all casual, but you can tell it bugs him that he doesn't really get it.

I offer, "GIF is a computer term. It's short for graphic

interchange format. It's a moving image on the internet—although some people pronounce it with a soft G: *jif*, like the peanut butter."

Malik glares at me. "No way the guy I'm cloned from used his dying breath to call me a graphics whatever. And he definitely didn't call me peanut butter. Those were his exact words: 'You're a giff.'"

Amber starts to laugh. "You're such a dummy, Malik! He didn't say *giff*. He said, 'You're a *gift!*' A long-lost son he never knew he had until the very end. He was telling you he *loved* you!"

Malik looks shocked, his face reddening as he realizes she must be right. He tries to shake it off, mumbling, "Yeah, right." But his eyes blink more than a few times.

I can't really tell you who moves first. But somehow the four of us end up in the middle of the room, clinging together like we never had the chance to do during all that time on the run. It's true that none of us has biological parents to love us. But we have each other, which is worth a lot more than some adult to pat you on the head when you bring home a good report card.

We also have Ms. Dunleavy. The only reason our new life works is that she's willing to do whatever it takes to erase our past and point us toward a real future. It's already cost her a lot to convince the people at Poseidon to keep silent about what happened in their lobby. And repairing the damage plus restocking the new aquarium with sea life won't be cheap either. The replacement manta ray alone has to be shipped from San Diego in a giant saltwater tank.

Ms. Dunleavy forgave us for stealing the Bentley—again—and sneaking off to Poseidon to rescue the other Osiris clones. She brought the eleven of us back to Jackson Hole to live on her estate. And the same deal she first offered Malik, Amber, Tori, and me—grow up, go to college, have real lives—now applies to the rest of us too.

There could never be a better person to share DNA with.

Malik's opinion: "Going from Bartholomew Glen to her is like upgrading to a Bentley." From him, there could be no higher compliment.

There's a catch, though: We have to pretend Project Osiris never happened. That means our parents, the other scientists, and the Purple People Eaters will go unpunished.

"Absolutely not!" is Amber's reaction. "They can't be allowed to get away with it!"

Ms. Dunleavy is patient. "I know it seems unfair, but you have to be reasonable. We've gone to great lengths to keep all this out of the media. If there are criminal trials of so many people, you kids will come to the attention of the whole world. The existence of eleven human clones will cause an instant sensation. It will put a spotlight on you that you won't be able to get away from. Then you'll never know the normal lives you fought so hard to have a chance at."

"I hate the idea of Project Osiris getting off scot-free," Tori muses. "But I can't stand the thought of my parents in jail, even if they deserve it." She flushes. "They were good to me. I can't help thinking, someday—you know, when I'm an adult, obviously—I might even be able to visit them."

We're split on that idea. Amber is a definite no; Hector too. Malik isn't so sure. He isn't so high on his dad, but he still talks about his mother's cooking all the time.

And me? I have no one. I never had a fake Serenity mom, and Felix Hammerstrom is dead. No one can argue that isn't a good thing. Yet I can't bring myself to celebrate it. He was the only parent I'll ever have.

Except Tamara Dunleavy.

She's not my mother, but we *are* related. In fact, our genetic connection is closer than any parent and child. I'm her and she's me.

Two computer nerds in a pod.

We start school in September—real school, with real teachers and real facts. Malik, Amber, and I are freshmen at Jackson Hole High School, along with Margaret, Robbie, Aldwin, and Ben. Tori, Hector, Freddie, and Penelope are eighth graders at the middle school, which is basically on the other side of our athletic field.

Malik's favorite part is the JV football program. "You're not just *allowed* to hit people; you're *supposed* to hit people, and as hard as you can. Man, we're not in Happy Valley anymore!"

He's definitely right on that score. When we learn about the American Revolution in social studies, I can't help but think back to the web page on Serenity's bogus internet about the Boston Tea Party:

> On December 16, 1773, American colonists met with representatives of the British government in Boston to discuss turning the thirteen colonies into a separate country. Tea was served.

That's honesty, harmony, and contentment for you. We weren't allowed to know about wars, revolts, or violence, so all that left was a friendly conversation over hot beverages.

I start to laugh, not just a chuckle, but loud, barking guffaws.

"Eli Frieden!" the teacher exclaims, horrified. "Control yourself!"

Control is out of the question. My laughter has a mind of its own. Tears of mirth stream down my cheeks. My sides ache. My entire body shakes. My student desk rocks on its uneven legs, thumping against the floor.

I get kicked out of class. So much for my spotless behavior record. On the other hand, who cares? I'm not the principal's son here.

Besides, laughing feels *so* good. I can't remember the last time I completely lost it like that. With my friend Randy, maybe. Randy. He's the only face from my former life I'd like to see again. It'll be tricky, because his parents are former Osiris researchers. Still, one day, years from now, I hope we can be friends again. If nothing else, I have to thank him. If it wasn't for Randy, I never would have taken the bike ride that turned into my first run-in with Serenity's invisible barrier. That was a horrible experience, but I'm grateful for it now. Without it, I might never have stumbled on the truth about Project Osiris.

We could all still be lab rats in the experiment.

* * *

One holdover from our old life—the eleven of us can't get enough information. After so many years in the Serenity bubble, we're all hungry for any kind of news we can find.

America's Most Wanted is doing a segment on none other than C. J. Rackoff, the notorious embezzler and con man. There are childhood pictures that look so much like Hector that everybody comments on it, even Ms. Dunleavy, who is watching with us.

No one knows where Rackoff is right now. There have been reports of him all over the world—including a recent sighting on the island of West Cay, Bahamas. That one, though, has never been officially confirmed.

According to the show, the most amazing thing about Rackoff is his spectacular breakout from the Kefauver prison in Texas. Corrections officials have no explanation for his escape, except to say that it must have been carried out by trained professionals.

That gets a big laugh in the TV room.

Well, I know for a fact that we're not professionals, and nobody trained us. Whatever skills we had in that break-out must have come from the DNA of the criminals we're cloned from.

That DNA is part of us, but it isn't all of us. It's something we've learned over these past months. If the point of Project Osiris was to prove that you're more than your genes, then the results are finally in.

We're not criminals. We're regular kids, like everybody else.

Still, you probably don't want to mess with us . . . just to be on the safe side.

GORDON KORMAN wrote his first book at age fourteen and since then has written more than eighty-five middle grade and teen novels. Favorites include the *New York Times* bestselling *The 39 Clues: Cahills vs. Vespers, Book One: The Medusa Plot*; *Ungifted*; *Pop*; and *Schooled*. Gordon is also the author of *Masterminds* and *Masterminds: Criminal Destiny*. He lives with his family on Long Island, New York. You can visit him online at www.gordonkorman.com.